Acclaim for KI Thompson's Books

House of Clouds

"...impressive first novel...wonderful characters, intrigue, history, and superb writing..." — *Just About Write*

"...*House of Clouds* envelops the reader in the drama of the Civil War and the intense passion of a woman's love story. Thompson shares her gift for vivid description with fascinating detail to make her characters and their struggles come alive...a good story that is both well-written and captivating." — Diane S. Isaacs, PhD in African American Studies, Professor, George Washington University Honors Program

"...KI Thompson has ventured into well-trodden ground, the American Civil War, and made it fresh and fascinating...It has the inevitability of a well-structured novel and the emotional delight of a troubadour's tale one wants to hear again and again. Welcome, Ms. Thompson, to the ranks of the writers. I look forward to your next book." — Ann Bannon, author of *The Beebo Brinker Chronicles*

"...Though essentially a love story, the novel very effectively takes on the issues of the mid-to-late 19th Century: slavery, race, culture, class, property, states' rights, relationships between men and women, and the taboos surrounding same-sex love. This epic saga moves along with great energy and clocks in at a delicious 377 pages. The author writes with surety and accomplishment, never allowing the historical events to take over the story. An engaging plot and lively characters...full of unexpected twists and turns. Highly recommended for all romance readers, lovers of historical fiction, and anyone who enjoys a fascinating story ably told." — *Midwest Book Review*

"...The historical facts of this epic time are skillfully interwoven with the fictional tale. That Thompson loves this era is obvious. That she can write complex characters into a compelling story is even more apparent. If you love historical fiction, don't miss *House of Clouds*. If you are new to it, try this one. It doesn't disappoint." — *Just About Write*

Heart of the Matter

"...a rich story, showing how love and friendship can grow despite superficial appearances, and that body image is in the eye of the beholder. Her characters are well developed, as is the love story. The sex is hot and vivid. *Heart of the Matter* is definitely a good read." — *Just About Write*

By the Author

House of Clouds

Heart of the Matter

Cooper's Deale

Visit us at www.boldstrokesbooks.com

COOPER'S
DEALE

by

KI Thompson

2008

ISBN 10: 1-60282-028-7
ISBN 13: 978-1-60282-028-9

This Trade Paperback Original Is Published By
Bold Strokes Books, Inc.
New York, USA

First Edition: September 2008

CREDITS
Editors: Shelley Thrasher and Stacia Seaman
Production Design: Stacia Seaman
Cover Design By Sheri (graphicartist2020@hotmail.com)

Acknowledgments

—

As always, my thanks go to Radclyffe for the opportunity to continue on this journey. It has been an extraordinary experience.

My heartfelt gratitude goes to my editor, Shelley Thrasher, who has been my guide through a maze of lessons that would take a novel to elucidate. That she can still tolerate me is nothing short of a miracle.

Thanks also go to Stacia Seaman for her tremendous attention to detail. I don't know how she does it.

Once again, Sheri has designed a terrific cover. Don't you ever run out of ideas?

My grudging praise goes to Kathi who made me go to Deale in the first place. Thanks; I think.

To the incredible women I've had the pleasure meeting online and through BSBauthorsconnect—you mean the world to me.

And finally, to readers everywhere who still love the feel of a book in their hands. Thank you.

Dedication

For Kathi, with all my love.

CHAPTER ONE

This element, P-u, was first detected in a cyclotron at Berkeley in 1940."

Francis James Gripp looked up from his work to see Alex Trebec on the television screen, perfectly groomed and coiffed, without a trace of perspiration. Frank had been examining the density gauge he had stolen from his job at the Department of Transportation. It measured the compaction of recently constructed roads and contained nuclear material.

"What is plutonium," Frank murmured at the television.

"How'd you know that, Frank?" Abel Gripp lit another cigarette with the burning stub of his last one.

Frank glanced at his brother, who was munching on a pepperoni pizza with their cousin Clarence. The contrast between his skinny, pock-marked kid brother and their lumbering-ox relative was striking. The only thing they had in common was their IQ, which ran in the negative numbers. While Frank also had a slender physique, he had supplemented his workouts with body building so that his muscles were more pronounced and his build more solid than Abel's.

"Learned it in the army," Frank replied, still absorbed by the gauge. He picked up a package of C-4, a plastic explosive, and removed it from the Baggie.

"Yeah, I bet they taught you a bunch of neat stuff about

blowing stuff up in the army, huh, Frank?" Clarence guffawed, then briefly choked on a mouthful of pizza. He held a beefy hand up to his mouth and hacked the contents into his palm.

Frank ignored his cousin. His pea brain couldn't comprehend the complexities of Frank's life in the military. Special Forces had indeed taught him much about explosives—and life. Frank figured he'd still be in the military, if it hadn't been for the so-called friendly-fire incident. His lieutenant had hated him and had intentionally detonated the munitions that cost him part of his right foot and a chunk of his thigh. The botched repair job at the VA hospital had left him almost crippled, but somehow, through sheer will, he had managed to walk again.

Suddenly something outside the window drew his attention from the claylike C-4. Rising from the kitchen table, he opened the back door on the warm, mid-June day and scanned the yard. He had been jittery the past few days, like someone was watching him. Searching the overgrown weeds that smothered the rusting, faded orange Allis-Chalmers tractor, he strained his ears but heard only the *Jeopardy* music in the background and a chirping Baltimore oriole, its orange underbelly contrasting sharply with the muddy greens and browns of the thicket.

The tractor made him recall a time when his father let him sit on his lap while he plowed the fields. It was one of his few positive memories. His parents were gone now, and his life in the military had forced him to leave the farm in the hands of his brother, who just let it go to pot. After a few minutes longer, he hobbled back to the kitchen.

"Angelina Jolie," Clarence burped out after chugging his Heineken.

"What is Angelina Jolie," the contestant responded.

"See, I told ya." Clarence jabbed Abel in the shoulder.

"Ow. But you didn't say 'What is.' You have to say 'What is Angelina Jolie.' Otherwise you lose."

Abel rubbed his shoulder. Clarence was a huge Neanderthal of a guy, with tufts of wiry black hair sticking out from his collar and shirt sleeves. Abel hated it when he punched him, even if he was just playing. He was always finding new bruises where Clarence's fist had landed.

"Nah, I could've had another shot and said, 'What is.'"

"I hate that. If you answer wrong, you shouldn't get a second chance. That's the one thing I hate about this show. People get a chance to correct themselves. It's not fair." Abel took his games seriously. He took a deep drag on his cigarette.

"Would you two shut the fuck up?" Frank said. "Take out these parts, Clarence, and burn them so there's nothing left. See if you can get that right."

Frank snagged a slice of pizza and limped into his office to the computer. He'd give part of his other foot to have the help of his buddy Wayne Newton. Not the singer, his army buddy. But Wayne was dead, his white grave marker at Arlington lost among the thousands of little grave markers that crowded the hillsides at the national cemetery. Wayne had been with him from boot camp to the Gulf War in '91, where a lucky shot from an Iraqi soldier nailed him. Stupid.

Now all he had was his idiot brother and, worse, their dimwitted cousin. His aunt had dumped Clarence and his equally moronic sister at their doorstep twenty-five years ago. She was somewhere in Vegas. She supposedly wanted to be a showgirl, but probably wound up prostituting herself on the Strip. Clarence's sister followed the circus as a concessionaire, handing out cheap plastic toys to anyone who managed to throw a ring around a Coke bottle. Nobody knew who their father was.

He sighed, bit into his pizza, and swigged his beer. Oh well, Abel and Clarence would have to do. They wouldn't be as effective as Wayne, but what Clarence lacked in brains he made up for in brawn. And Abel always did what Frank told him.

The brains part of this job belonged to him anyway. It was his plan, his idea. And he was doing this for Wayne, in his memory. Well, he was doing this for himself too. *Goddamn government*. If it wasn't for them, he would still have his foot and leg intact, and

Wayne would still be alive. They owed him. He logged into eBay and searched for any sales of uranium. He smiled inwardly at the current bid on an auction for uranium-238: easily affordable at less than $20. Thirty-one grams of uranium was enough, he hoped.

Clarence hauled the pieces of wiring and used parts Frank had thrown away to the barrel out back. Of all the crap Frank had forced him to do the last two years, he hated this the most. When he reached the blackened barrel, he hurled the stuff into it and knocked it over backward, like he'd done a few times in the past months. Some of the parts tumbled down into the water and disappeared in the murky depths of the Chesapeake Bay.

If he couldn't see it, nobody else could, so he righted the barrel and dumped the rest of the trash inside. After dousing the garbage with some gasoline, he lit a cigarette and stood back. When he tossed the match inside the barrel he felt the whoosh of air as the parts ignited.

❖

Meanwhile, across the bay, Tommy Cooper sat hunched over in the safety of his home, a neat tree house in the top of a huge red oak on his grandmother's farm. The loblolly pines that dotted the rest of the shore nearly ruined his view of the house across the inlet, but not quite. Using his green plastic binoculars, he watched the three men who came and went all day.

The man in camouflage reminded him of a snipe, the big hairy one a pelican, and the skinny guy a sandpiper. But why did that other man, in a tan shirt and blue jeans, spend most of his time up to his knees in the murky waters behind a rusty old tractor? The crane—that's what he called him—acted like he was playing hide-and-seek with the three men in the house. But they weren't very good at the game. Right now one of them came to the door but didn't even leave the porch. He just went back inside. Stupid.

The man in the tan shirt was carrying something, and Tommy squinted through his binoculars to see what it was. A warm breeze made the tops of the pines sway and dance, and they blocked his view for a minute. When the breeze died down, he could tell that the man had a camera and was taking pictures.

The crane stalked through the water and weeds, stepping with his long legs slowly along the water's edge. Any minute he might dive into the water and spear a fish. He was quick, but he didn't seem to mind waiting for hours in the hot sun.

The big pelican had come out of the house and was burning stuff in a barrel. Tommy laughed every time this happened. It was almost as good as the Fourth of July fireworks—especially when the barrel fell over and the pelican hopped around and kicked it. It was as interesting as the time Jeff Olson thought he got cooties from a girl who kissed him on Valentine's Day.

Jeff was his best friend, and Tommy helped him get the cooties off with some spit and sandpaper. Jeff's kite getting stuck in Tommy's tree made them become buddies. When Jeff climbed the tree to get it down, Tommy nearly ran away. He was afraid Jeff would make fun of him. But Jeff liked his cool house and wanted to be his best friend.

"Tommy Jay Cooper, it's suppertime." His grandmother always bothered him when he was having fun.

"Aw, Grandma, not now. Something really interesting is goin' on over there. Can I eat later?"

"You'll eat now or I'll be up that tree and whup you in a New York minute, boy. I'm not that old. I used to climb trees all the time, when your grandpa was off plowing the fields." She rested on the stump at the base of the oak and placed Tommy's supper in the metal bucket tied by a rope to a tree branch. "Those were the days, back when we had over two hundred acres of corn, some good broilers, and four cows. We didn't need nothin' back then. And what we did need, we sold our grain and paid cash for at Hadley's store. Mind my words, boy—no credit. Never needed credit."

"Credit's bad," Tommy replied, like he was supposed to.
"Darn tootin'."

She finished placing the meal in the bucket and Tommy hoisted it up. As it went up, a flash of bright light reflecting off the bucket blinded her. Closing her eyes, she stepped away from the tree and out into the open yard. When she opened them again, she shaded her eyes with her hand and blinked up at the sky, trying to see through the white splotches.

A deafening roar came out of nowhere and she slowly turned in circles, trying to understand what was happening. Something was blocking the sun now and heading right for her. She started to run to get out from under it, thinking it must be an airplane.

CHAPTER TWO

Addy Cooper sat at her cheap gray metal desk, a spreadsheet open on her computer. She tried to make sense of the numbers, twisting a clump of her unruly hair, then blinked rapidly to clear her fuzzy vision. She had worked and reworked the columns all morning and still couldn't quite balance the accounts. Something was missing. Peeping through the blinds at her window, she glimpsed the sun setting over the buildings along San Francisco Bay.

"More coffee?"

She swiveled to see the receptionist hovering in the doorway, holding an almost-empty pot of coffee.

"No thanks." Addy groaned. "I'll be up all night as it is."

"It's after five. I'm leaving. Aren't you going home?"

Addy sighed. "I wish. But I can't leave until the books are done. Have a good weekend."

She returned to her spreadsheet, but a few seconds later she noticed the little clock on her screen. Maureen would be pissed, especially since this was Friday. The demands of Addy's job annoyed her partner, and they fought endlessly over it. About to reach for the phone and dreading the call she'd have to make, she heard a loud scuffle in the lobby. She and a few other employees headed there.

A group of men in suits fanned out through the office, jerking file cabinets open and entering employee offices. Addy's boss was bent over the reception desk as one man handcuffed him and read his Miranda rights.

"What's going on?" The scene bewildered Addy.

"FBI." An agent flashed his ID. "No one is to leave the building while we search the premises." He motioned two agents to the back wall, where several black metal filing cabinets stood. The agents began to dump the files into boxes marked "Evidence."

"Do you have a warrant?" Addy asked the question automatically, reacting to the events unfolding before her and having viewed too many episodes of *Law and Order*. She had little idea of the legal issues involved.

The agent who had identified himself stared at her. He hitched up his pants, but gravity, and the circumference of his belly, kept them up only temporarily. "Who wants to know?"

"I'm Addy Cooper." Her voice cracked, betraying her exterior calm. "I work here, and that's our boss you're handcuffing. What's he being accused of?"

He reached into his inside jacket pocket and removed a packet of papers. Unfolding them and holding them up, he moved closer, invading her personal space. She didn't want to appear intimidated, so she stood her ground but leaned back slightly.

"Here's your warrant, Ms. Cooper. We're confiscating Wor Import Export property on suspicion of illegal activity involving the black market. We suspect your boss is importing Russian brides and exporting bootleg copies of prereleased movies. What exactly is your role here?"

"I'm an accountant." Addy began to tremble as she realized the seriousness of the crime. She had met many Russian-speaking women through her boss, who explained that they were friends or relatives visiting from abroad. She rarely encountered them again and thought nothing of it. As for videos or DVDs, hundreds of boxes left the warehouse daily, but she assumed they contained machine parts.

"We'll need to question you too, Ms. Cooper. The rest of you return to your offices. You will be interviewed and released as soon as possible."

The other employees of Wor Import Export shuffled away, a few warily staring over a shoulder at Addy. The agent who appeared to be in charge of the raid led her into the first office off the lobby.

Once more Addy chanced a peek at the clock on the wall and sighed. Yup, Maureen was going to be really pissed. Her shoulders sagged and she suddenly felt a hundred years old. Would life ever get any better than this?

❖

If Liberty McDonald loved one thing, it was seeing justice done. She hung back in the crowd of onlookers as the Chicago PD and fellow FBI agents hauled the bad guys away. The longer Special Agent Jerry Cruikshank talked to the media, the more her temper rose. Jerry would claim all the credit for the arrest, even though her undercover activity had nailed the bastards. Besides, she looked better in front of the camera than he did. *What a slob*. It might help if he invested in a decent suit. The camera loved her strong features and devilish grin. And the ladies regarded her pretty highly as well.

Liberty couldn't suppress a broad grin as the suspect was led out of the building. Of all the assholes being arrested today, he was the one she was most proud of nailing. The greedy kingpin was responsible for dumping toxic waste directly into Lake Michigan—had told his drivers to back the trucks up there at night to get rid of his company's chemical waste. God knew how much damage he had caused by the time she was assigned the job of discovering the source of the pollution.

As he walked by, she reflexively shrank back, not wanting him to recognize her and possibly put the pieces together regarding her involvement. But she really wanted to grab the bastard and beat the shit out of him. The poor flora and fauna. It would take years of work to restore the area. *Scum like that ought to be taken out back and shot. Screw the trial.*

Her cell phone rang and she moved far enough away not to be heard.

"Liberty."

"When this is over, we need you in Maryland. Spend what time you need there closing out that case, then fly out to Baltimore. Pick up a rental car there, and it's about two hours to Deale."

"What's up?"

"You'll get the details later, but there's unusual activity along that area of the Chesapeake. Radioactive elements in the water supply. They're not at high levels yet, but they're recent, within the past couple of months, and seem to be increasing. Some local reporter says he has information relevant to the case—possibly a terrorist threat. Hook up with him when you get there. Again, that will all be in the file."

"Okay. Anything else?"

"We don't know what we're dealing with, so be careful."

"Always."

Liberty flipped the phone shut and shook her head. Guys like her handler always warned, "Be careful." Easy for them to say, being tucked away in some cushy darkened room on the phone all day. They never stuck their necks out, never had to worry about looking over their shoulder all the time. But she'd be bored out of her skull with a job like that. She needed the outdoors more than she needed sex, and that was saying a lot—not that she ever had to worry about getting any.

She sauntered down the street toward her car parked several blocks away. Passing a shop window, she paused to check out her reflection. Her jeans were perfect—tight and just the right shade of faded blue. They accentuated her muscular thighs and narrow waist, and she tucked her shirt in where it had come out. Satisfied that everything was strategically placed the way she liked it, she finger-combed her hair and resumed walking.

❖

Back in California Addy and the other employees weren't released from their temporary confinement until almost ten o'clock. Her boss had been taken away long ago. What would become of him, and what would become of her job? She told the others she would try to find out more from the FBI in the morning and call them.

Heading out of Alameda in her blue Volvo, she considered calling Maureen as she crossed the bridge into Oakland, but knew it wouldn't matter. Maureen could care less what the explanation would be this time. She would haughtily toss her thick red curls and point a polished fingernail at her, saying Addy loved her job more than she loved her. Lately, Addy had begun to believe her.

The lights inside were on and she knew Maureen was waiting. After she parked, a knot formed in her gut and with each step her body tensed. Four pieces of luggage and several boxes greeted her in the entryway.

"Maureen?"

She dropped her briefcase on the floor and entered the living room, where Maureen sat on the couch, arms folded across her chest.

"I can explain," Addy weakly began.

Maureen held up her hand, signaling her unwillingness to listen.

"I've had enough," she said. "BJ will be here any minute. If I missed anything or if I get any mail, I've left you an address to forward them."

"Who's BJ?" The abruptness of Maureen's declaration stunned Addy.

Before Maureen could answer, the doorbell rang and she ran to answer it.

"Hey, babe." A short, muscular woman wearing the brown shirt and shorts of a UPS driver wrapped a meaty arm around Maureen's waist. Maureen quickly squirmed her way out of the woman's grasp, brushing a loose red curl back into place.

"BJ, this is Addy." Maureen gestured.

"You're leaving me for her?" How could Maureen toss her aside so casually—and for a UPS driver, no less? Maureen had clearly been more than just a parcel recipient to the butch woman. This second shock of the day staggered Addy.

"BJ has regular hours and gets paid big bucks for any overtime *she* works," Maureen said. "I'm tired of sitting around waiting for you every night while you waste your life in that dreary, dead-end job. I want more out of life."

"So you've opted for the excitement that only a UPS driver can give you."

"Don't be snide, Addy. I've taken all the crap I can from you these last four years. I hope you enjoy your miserable life. Come on, BJ, let's go."

Maureen picked up the luggage while BJ easily hefted the large boxes and dropped them onto a waiting dolly outside the door.

Addy stood in the entryway long after the front door had slammed, the silence unnerving. Although the house was small, it suddenly felt cavernous. She stared at the walls, hoping they'd provide an answer to her dilemma. But she was exhausted, too drained to worry about the future.

She dragged herself up the stairs and into their bedroom, the bed and dressers in disarray from Maureen's hasty departure. The mess left Addy's orderly brain unsettled. She smoothed the bedspread out, picked up a few articles of clothing from the floor and put them away, then walked to the closet.

Every aching bone in her body cried out for sleep. She undressed, hanging her skirt and jacket neatly on their hangers, placed her pumps on the shoe rack, toes pointing inward, and climbed into bed. The cool sheets calmed her and she instantly relaxed.

Where was Maureen moving? Maureen was on her health insurance plan at work. Monday, she would ask personnel to remove her name from both the health and life insurance policies. Maureen would probably get better coverage with UPS anyway.

CHAPTER THREE

The phone rang at seven o'clock and Addy fumbled for the receiver.

"Hello?"

"Addy? It's Karen Kaczarowski. I mean, this is Officer Kaczarowski. I'm calling on official business."

When Addy heard Karen's voice, the sleepy fog inside her brain cleared instantly. *Karen Kaczarowski.* She hadn't heard her name in ages. But Addy had thought about her occasionally. Her voice, even after all these years, made her shiver. It was as though they had spoken only yesterday.

"What is it, Officer?" Addy questioned stiffly. Karen couldn't possibly think she could simply call and Addy would crawl back to her. Karen had betrayed her, and she would never forget that.

"I'm sorry to be the one to bring you bad news, Addy. Your grandmother passed away yesterday."

Addy gasped, her hand flying to her throat. "What happened?"

"I arrived at the scene at six fifteen p.m.," Karen recited, as though reading from notes. "A neighbor phoned to say that she had found Adelaide Cooper, your grandmother, dead in the backyard of her home. A large piece of space debris, approximately thirty-six by twenty-five by eighteen inches, evidently killed her. Authorities are examining the object to determine its origin, but initial assessments identify it as a piece of communications equipment from a Russian Soyuz orbital module. That's all we have at the moment."

"What about Tommy?" Addy's heart thumped wildly. Dazed, she didn't ask herself what else could go wrong because, with her luck, anything could happen.

"He's okay. He's still up in his tree, but keeps asking where his grandma is. Mrs. Sweetwater from next door and, uh, I are keeping an eye on him."

Addy sat up and swung her legs to the floor, then shoved her hand into her hair and scratched her head roughly, trying to clear her mind. *Poor Grandma.* Her eyes burned and she swallowed convulsively. She didn't want to cry, at least not with Karen on the phone.

"Are you all right, Addy?"

"I'm fine." Addy wanted no sympathy from Karen. She was still angry at her. The intensity of her pain had lessened over the years, but a small flicker of resentment still lingered. She was surprisingly glad, though, to hear Karen's voice and was comforted that Karen had called, rather than some stranger who didn't know Tommy or understand his special needs.

"I'll see if I can get a flight out today and will let you know when I'll arrive. Please tell Tommy that I'm coming and to not be afraid."

"I'd be happy to pick you up at the airport."

"No, thank you. I need to rent a car anyway."

It was so tempting to let Karen take care of her again, especially now that she had so much to do and think about. What would she do with her brother? He would never survive the move from Maryland to California. The farm where he grew up was all he knew, and she couldn't possibly ask him to leave his tree house. What would the farm bring? The house was nearly a hundred years old. What state of repair was it in?

"Well, okay. Call me so I can tell Tommy."

"I will."

Unable to get a flight the same day, she booked an early morning flight from Oakland to Baltimore. She had a quick shower and a cup of coffee, packed enough clothes for two weeks, and with the rest of the afternoon to kill, drove into Alameda to the office. She wanted to find out more about what was going on, but the yellow tape across the door and a large chain with a padlock told her all she needed to know. She obviously wouldn't have to worry about work on Monday.

Still, she needed to confirm exactly what was happening. She dug into her purse for her cell phone and the business card of the FBI agent who had interrogated her. When he didn't answer, she left a message.

She returned home, still in shock over her grandmother's death. Her grandmother had taken care of her and her brother for fifteen years, ever since their anthropologist parents were reported missing in the Amazon jungle. Addy was ten years old, and her brother Tommy was seven. He had climbed up into the oak tree and he never came down from it, clearly believing that he was a bird and the tree house his nest. Addy believed it was his way of dealing with the loss.

He didn't seem to remember their parents at all, and even Addy retained only shimmering memories. Were they in fact actual recollections or fantasies she had created of what she wished to remember? The faded photographs in family albums revealed a rather clownish couple wearing a vast array of tribal attire, from headgear to footwear.

As a child, Addy had giggled at the funny images, but now they appeared ridiculous. Her parents had been foolhardy, which had probably caused their death. Why couldn't they have been more like real parents and gone to an office every day, or stayed home and baked cookies like her grandmother?

Addy's throat tightened and her eyes burned. Her grandmother had been her entire world. Even living in California and being with Maureen, Addy had still considered Deale her home. Now that she and Tommy were alone, she would have to create a new home for them, one where Tommy would feel equally safe and loved. She only hoped she could be as strong and competent as her grandmother.

❖

When the gentle chime alerted passengers of the plane's descent into BWI, Addy looked up from *CPA Today* and out the window. The plane circled the city and the harbor that prevented its further expansion east.

She was coming home for only the second time in almost seven years. She had meant to go off to college for a few years, returning for summer vacations, then move back permanently after she graduated.

But she met Maureen, a cheerleader at Berkeley, and within weeks had moved in with her in a rush of hormonal necessity.

Grandma Adelaide, Addy's namesake, supported her desire to stay in California. Jobs were far more plentiful and better paying there. Addy needed to make her own way in life, her grandmother said. She was young and didn't need to take care of her brother. That would come soon enough.

But the frequent checks Addy sent home for Tommy's support didn't help assuage her guilt over abandoning him. The one time she had visited, Maureen had come with her. She despised everything about Deale, and they never returned.

Addy didn't like to think about her other reason for leaving Maryland—Karen Kaczarowski. They had known each other since Karen's family moved from Fort Meade to Deale. Karen had made Addy laugh on the first day of second grade, and they became instant best friends. All the way through high school they shared everything, including birthdays and life events, both momentous and mundane.

But in their junior year they discovered they were more than simply friends. Addy would never forget their first kiss, which was unlike anything she had experienced before or since. They were in love from the very beginning, and it made the infidelity all the more painful.

Addy had been hunting Karen after gym class during third period one day. The hot shower had made her horny, and she needed the release that Karen was always willing to provide. Merely the idea of Karen's hands roaming her heated flesh aroused her. In her rush to find her, she hadn't knocked on Miss Wilson's office door and had burst in upon them.

At first the scene in front of her didn't make sense. Why did Karen fall off Miss Wilson's desk and fumble with her jeans, pulling them up from around her ankles? Perhaps Karen had injured herself during volleyball, so Addy moved toward her to see if she could help. But something in Miss Wilson's rugged, confident face made her stop, an expression she had never seen on her—embarrassment. Then it dawned on Addy—Karen and Miss Wilson were having sex.

The airplane's touchdown jolted Addy from her reverie. When they arrived at the gate and the "fasten seat belts" light had been turned off, she gathered her belongings, neatly folded her navy blue blanket, and followed the signs to Hertz.

❖

The airline's Web site announced that Addy's plane had arrived on time, so in less than two hours Addy would be in Deale. Karen already had sweaty palms.

She had never stopped thinking about Addy. She had screwed up their relationship back in high school and felt guilty ever since. And while she felt terrible about Addy's grandmother, she was excited about seeing Addy again. She had always fantasized that they would get back together and hoped they could at least reconcile.

"Hey, Karen, call on line two."

Karen punched the button on her desk phone. "Deputy Kaczarowski."

"Deputy? It's Myrna Sweetwater."

"Yes, Mrs. Sweetwater. Is something wrong with Tommy?"

"No, dear, he's fine. Though when I took his lunch earlier, he flapped his arms and ran around the tree house with his usual 'Caw! Caw!' I'm guessing he didn't like the grilled-cheese sandwich and tomato soup. I hoped they would comfort him."

"Ravens don't like tomato soup. But I'll bet he ate the grilled cheese."

"Why, mercy me. Yes, he did. Left only the crusts. How'd you guess?"

Karen smiled into the phone. "When you're around Tommy long enough, you begin to realize these things."

"Well, he was asking for you again. He seems to be a little more unsettled than usual."

"I can imagine." Change upset Tommy. When his parents were reported missing, something inside his brain had snapped. The stability of his grandmother's care had kept him from completely disengaging from society, although Addy's departure had obviously affected him deeply, even though she called and wrote him every week.

Karen couldn't blame him. Addy's absence had upset her too. She could almost feel the sting on her face from the slap Addy had left her with. Her own guilt hadn't helped matters either.

"Kaczarowski, come here for a sec."

Karen's boss stood in the doorway of his office, and she waved her acknowledgement.

"I've got to go, Mrs. Sweetwater. But tell Tommy I'll be over later. We'll have dinner when his sister arrives."

She hung up the phone and strode to the office.

"Yeah, Chief?"

"Got someone on their way to see you." He tossed her a file. "FBI. Coming out to investigate something going on around here. Something to do with the dead fish we've been seeing lately."

"InfraGard?"

InfraGard was a collaborative effort between institutions of higher learning, commercial enterprises, various levels of law enforcement, and Homeland Security to prevent hostile acts against the United States. Karen had become a member a few years ago as part of her involvement with law enforcement, but also because of her love of the Chesapeake. She flipped through the file, scanning the documents.

"Yup. I'm putting you on it. But this agent is undercover, so only you and I will know why they're here. If it's terrorists, we need to find them, and find them fast."

CHAPTER FOUR

Deale, Maryland, was a small community, less than five thousand people, on the Western Shore of the Chesapeake Bay. The town provided plenty of charter fishing boats, primarily for residents from the Annapolis and Washington, DC, areas.

But for Addy Cooper, Deale had been the perfect playground for long hot summers spent getting a tan on the dock behind her house. With Tommy perpetually ensconced in his tree house and Karen rubbing Coppertone sensuously over her body, all had seemed right in the world. Addy could have stayed that way forever and wanted for nothing, until the "incident."

She had been angry at Karen for a very long time—for her loss of innocence in Miss Wilson's office and for the loss of her few memories of happiness. Could she face Karen now, after all this time, and pretend that nothing had happened? Perhaps she had forgotten the entire incident. Just the possibility made her angry.

Driving into Deale, Addy turned onto Masons Beach Road and from there onto Parkers Creek Drive. Vacation homes had sprung up throughout the area, driving housing prices up and crowding the open spaces that had once abounded. All that was left of her grandparents' large farm was several acres of land and the rambling house. It had so many additions that its original style had been totally obscured.

A county sheriff's car sat on the street out front when Addy pulled into the driveway, and her heart rate accelerated. *Karen.* She should have known her ex would be waiting.

She left her luggage in the car and hesitantly climbed the steps to the front door. This was home, and she should just walk right in. But something held her back. Was she still welcome here? How would Tommy react to her? Would he be angry at her for leaving? Would he refuse to come with her, and if so, what would she do with him?

Before she could make up her mind, the door opened and Officer Karen Kaczarowski stood there. Addy's mind turned to mush and her bones felt like rubber. *Damn!* Karen looked hot in that uniform. She was slender and athletic, solid yet not bulky, her dark blue eyes swirling with emotion Addy couldn't quite decipher.

"Addy," Karen murmured. "It's so good to see you again."

"Officer," Addy managed to say. She refused to call her Karen. It seemed too intimate and she wouldn't give her the satisfaction. Addy planned to maintain a businesslike atmosphere and convey only what needed to be said. The less time she spent in the presence of this—this betrayer, the better. Karen probably didn't even remember that she had never apologized for the affair.

"Tommy's out back, of course. Come on in." She opened the door wider.

Addy resented the movement, as though Karen lived there and should be inviting Addy into her own home. Her grandmother had shown Addy a copy of her will long ago, bequeathing the house and land to her upon her death. But Addy hadn't expected her to die so soon.

Thinking of her grandmother, and seeing all of her possessions just as they had always been brought a lump to Addy's throat. She didn't get a chance to say good-bye.

She had spoken to her grandmother the week before her death but had been in a hurry. Work had been pressing down on her, and at the end of the phone conversation, she had forgotten to say "I love you," like she always did. Addy was appalled to feel a tear trickle down the side of her nose.

"Hey, it's going to be all right." Karen put her arms around her, but Addy jerked away.

"I want to see Tommy." She hurried around Karen, avoiding her like an animal avoids stepping in its own waste. Besides, Karen's arms felt too good to let them linger longer than necessary.

When she walked out the back door onto the screened-in porch that faced Parkers Creek, the beauty and tranquility of the sun setting over the water washed through her and she relaxed for the first time since she had touched down at BWI. The big red oak was lush and thick with leaves, providing a deep shade over the wooden picnic table where she and Karen had sat when they ate together. She could distinguish the tree house hidden among the branches and knew that Tommy was somewhere inside. Taking a deep breath, she entered the yard.

"Tommy?"

Footsteps on the floorboards above told her he had heard and was probably peeking down at her right now. His window was open and she called up to him.

"Tommy, it's me, Addy. I'm home."

"Caw! Caw! Big deal."

She winced. His response shouldn't have surprised her, but it did. And it hurt worse than she had anticipated. She approached the tree cautiously, then began to climb the ladder as Tommy leaned out the window and peered down at her, flapping his arms as though about to take flight.

"Go away, Addy. I'm mad at you."

"I know, sweetie, I know. And I'm sorry. It doesn't make up for my time away, but now I'm home, and I'm not leaving you again. Okay?" She pulled herself up to the door of the small enclosure and respectfully knocked. "Can I come in?"

"No."

"Please? I just want to talk to you about Grandma."

A moment of silence greeted her pronouncement, and then she heard the lock turn in the door. She ducked at the entryway, then stood up in the one-room enclosure. Tommy sat on his bed, his hands folded neatly in his lap. He gazed at her with the eyes of a wounded animal, which broke her heart.

"Oh, Tommy." In three steps she was by his side. He flung himself into her outstretched arms and clung to her, sobbing into her neck.

"Shh, honey. Addy's here. Don't worry. I'm never leaving you again."

"They say Grandma's dead, Addy. They say I can't see her no more."

"I know, sweetie, I know. But I'm home and I'll take care of you now."

She cried along with him and understood for the first time what it was like to be an orphan. No adults were left to care for her and Tommy. She was the grownup now, and she had to be the strong one.

"I'm hungry." Tommy sniffed, wiping his face on his sleeve.

Addy smiled through her tears. "Okay, then. What would you like for dinner?"

"Worms."

"You can't have worms, but you can have pizza."

"Okay."

She clambered down the tree and was startled to discover Karen waiting at the picnic table. The combination of sun and shade left a freckled pattern across her face, and she had never been more handsome. Her dark hair and light eyes, and her olive complexion dark from exposure to the sun, made Addy shiver. But the dull ache in her heart that had never completely healed resurfaced. What might have been in their relationship haunted her.

"I hope you don't mind," Karen said softly, "but I've been

staying at the house until you got here. Just to make sure Tommy was okay."

"No, I don't mind at all. I'm glad he wasn't alone. I hope it wasn't an imposition." Addy leaned against the picnic table but refused to sit down. It would seem too much like old times, and she didn't want to remember their old times.

"I was glad to do it. In fact, since you've been gone, Tommy and I have become good friends. I like to spend time with him. He's a great kid."

Addy was surprised. Karen had always been good with Tommy, even when they were children. She would defend him from all the bullies who made fun of him and even wound up with a black eye on occasion. Addy was grateful that Karen had continued the friendship despite the end of their relationship. She was also even guiltier that Karen, not her, had been taking care of Tommy.

"Well, I'm back now so you don't have to do that anymore. Thanks for looking out for him." She pushed off from the table. "I need to make his dinner now. Thanks again."

Addy wanted her to go away—rather, her libido wanted her to go away—but Karen didn't seem to take the hint.

"I want to help, Addy. The past is the past. Stop punishing us for a stupid mistake that happened a long time ago."

The bile roiled up from Addy's gut. "Mistake? You call cheating on me with Miss Wilson a mistake? A mistake is using a ballpoint pen to do a crossword puzzle. You broke my heart—no, you tore my heart out of my chest and stomped on it."

She was losing control and was shocked that all the feelings she had considered buried long ago rushed so quickly to the surface. But she couldn't cure the festering wound.

Karen jumped up. "Addy, you haven't changed one bit. You're still the same old tight-ass—and I don't mean that in a good way—and bitter woman who left here over six years ago. I hope you're happy in your misery, but don't spread it around."

Addy watched her stalk away. Talk about tight asses. Even

in her fury she admired the flex of muscle in Karen's butt that the clinging pants of her uniform couldn't hide. When the patrol car revved up and skidded angrily away, she felt suddenly deflated.

She hadn't wanted to reveal so many feelings in her first encounter with Karen. She had planned to display only dispassionate indifference that would hopefully inflict a mortal wound, like the one Karen had inflicted on her. Instead, she had only deepened her own pain.

❖

Karen parked in the lot across the street from the Happy Harbor Inn and went inside. The usual crowd was in the bar—local bikers and a few weathered fishermen—drinking beer and yelling at a game on the television. She found a stool and plopped down.

"Evenin', Karen. Off duty?" The bartender, Dee-Dee Lovelace, greeted her. When Karen nodded, Dee-Dee grabbed a bottle of Wild Turkey from the shelf and poured a long shot, setting it in front of Karen.

"Hey, Dee-Dee." Karen downed the shot in one large gulp. The heat spread quickly and she relaxed a bit, but it would take a lot more than one drink to ease her anger.

"How's Tommy doing?" Dee-Dee poured another one.

"He'll be fine. Addy's here."

"Addy? She is? That's great. I can't wait to see her. Geez, how long has it been?"

"Over six years, almost seven now, I guess." Karen tossed the second shot back, and this time she really felt it.

"Wow. Time flies. So…are you okay?"

Karen eyed her warily. Dee-Dee had been a friend to both her and Addy in high school, but she had been Addy's best friend first. Addy had shared everything with Dee-Dee, including the Miss Wilson fiasco.

"I'm fine. She'll probably swing by here at some point. But I can tell you right now, she hasn't changed one iota since she left. She still hates me."

"Oh, come on, now. That's ancient history. She can't possibly hold a grudge that long." Dee-Dee raised the bottle and Karen held up a finger for one more.

"Guess again." This time Karen sipped the liquor as it burned throughout her bloodstream.

The moment she'd laid eyes on Addy, the old feelings had washed over her like a gentle summer rain. She was mad at herself for not being able to clear up the Miss Wilson thing long ago. It really had been a mistake. The woman had seduced her, and she had let her hormones get the best of her. Besides, Miss Wilson had an experienced mouth that could do incredible things and she had let go of her inhibitions, even knowing what she was doing was wrong. Of all people to walk in on them, it had to be Addy.

When Addy had told her she'd be coming home, Karen secretly hoped they could patch things up. And when she saw her, her body said yes. But her brain was beginning to doubt the possibility. Addy had never forgiven her and probably never would. Fine. She had always been able to find comfort in the arms of various women in town. She didn't need the complications that Addy presented. She'd be around for a couple of weeks and then would probably return to California. Good riddance.

CHAPTER FIVE

Addy carried her luggage upstairs to her old room, though she had contemplated putting it in the master bedroom on the main floor. But she couldn't bring herself to go into her grandmother's room yet. Addy couldn't imagine life without her. The way her grandmother had died made her shudder. What were the odds of being hit by a piece of space debris?

Her own room was exactly as she had left it six years ago. Nothing was out of place because she hadn't left anything personal in the room except the furniture and quilt on the bed. Addy had removed her collection of photographs and stuffed animals, mementos of the time she had spent with Karen, before she left, not wanting any reminders of that painful time in her life.

Exhausted from her trip, she quickly unpacked. Methodically, she placed lingerie in the top drawer of her dresser and slacks and blouses in the closet, all color coordinated, and then ran a bath. Even though it had been years since she had been in the house, she instinctively turned the cold-water tap for hot water and the hot for cold. She submerged herself in the claw-foot tub, luxuriating in its depth. The warm water relaxed her, and her mind drifted to the last twenty-four hours.

Losing Maureen was the least of her troubles. Their relationship had been less than satisfying, especially during the last two years. But Addy had hung on, avoiding the confrontation and histrionics Maureen inevitably introduced any time Addy said she was unhappy.

She hadn't expected the UPS driver, however. Even now, the idea of Maureen cheating on her conjured up all the old anger and insecurities she'd felt with Karen. And seeing Karen only magnified the feelings. But her body's betrayal really shocked her, because she had believed those urges were long dead and buried. Squirming in the tepid water, she tried to ease the discomfort the memory caused. She sat up and turned the tap to warm the rapidly cooling water.

She really needed to focus on what was important right now—funeral plans and Tommy's future. Her savings would tide her over for a while, but now that she'd lost her job, she'd have to decide what to do with her own life as well. And soon.

❖

Frank's gut told him someone was watching the house, yet each time he went out into the yard to check things out, he couldn't see anybody. But the odd sensation persisted. Something just wasn't right. A few days ago, he could swear he heard metal clanging against metal out by the old tractor. Though he started to investigate, the ache in his leg prevented him from climbing down the hill to the water line. Later, he'd sent Abel to check it out, but he hadn't found anything.

Yesterday had been so quiet—not even the wind blew in the trees—and he might have heard a camera shuttering, but was pretty sure he'd imagined it. His instincts had always served him well and had saved his ass more than once in the Gulf. He sat in the dark, waiting by the window, and peeked out. The half-moon provided very little light, but his training had honed his night vision, and he only needed to be patient.

"See anything, Frank?" Abel asked on a puff of smoke.

"Quiet," he snarled.

Abel sat in the dark and sulked. They hadn't been able to turn on the television or play cards for hours now, yet each time he or Clarence fell asleep, Frank kicked them awake. Frank was probably being paranoid, but Frank was always paranoid. Ever since he came home from the war, he had been a little odd. But Abel knew as long as he did what Frank said, he'd be fine.

"Ain't nothin' but crickets," Clarence whispered in Abel's ear. "Frank's crackin' up."

"Better not tell him that," Abel whispered back. "You don't want to make him mad."

"I ain't afraid of him. Hey!"

Frank kicked Clarence as hard as he could.

"Shut up, you idiot. I'm in charge, and you'll do as I say or you can crawl back to Vegas and try to find your mommy."

"You'd better not say anything bad about my mother, Frank." Clarence stood up from his place on the floor, clenching his fists and shaking.

"Or what? You gonna beat me up, huh, Clarence? Try it, I dare you. Just try it. You'll wish you'd never been born to that whore."

Clarence slammed a fist into Frank's face, sending him crashing into the rocking chair by the window. He jumped on top of Frank, and they rolled over and over on the hardwood floor, knocking over table lamps and punching each other without doing much damage.

While Abel sort of agreed with Clarence that Frank was losing it, and while Clarence was twice as big as he was, he knew better than to go against his own brother. Not because he was blood kin, but because, unlike Clarence, he was afraid of Frank. Sighing, he jumped onto Clarence's back and joined in.

❖

Scott Vinson crouched beneath the living room window and released his breath. For a desperate minute he was afraid he had been discovered, but peeping through the glass, he could distinguish shadows moving inside, apparently fighting. He had tracked Frank Gripp through paper trails from his job at the Department of Transportation, which he had left six months ago, to his family's house on the Chesapeake in the part of Anne Arundel known as South County.

Scott, an investigative journalist with *The Deale Picayune*, was working on a piece involving twelve density gauges that had disappeared from the department gradually over the course of eight years. That was much more than just a misplaced piece or two of equipment.

While not significant by themselves, the recent thefts had led a few knowledgeable scientists to comment about the minute quantity of radioactive material in each gauge. The scientists, members of the National Nuclear Security Administration, were tasked with retrieving these stolen pieces of equipment and returning them to their rightful place. It dawned on them that, in large quantities, these seemingly innocent objects could be used as dirty bombs. Even one gauge, put in a box with an explosive, while not capable of harming many people outright, would cause enough mayhem and billions in cleanup to warrant concern.

Digging deeper into the problem, Scott had discovered that over the past few years, thousands of pieces of equipment containing radioactive materials had gone missing nationwide from various businesses and government agencies. No one seemed to know where they had gone, and what was worse, no one seemed to care. Scott convinced his editor to give him some time off, and he immediately set out to find what was happening with equipment missing from the Department of Transportation. He was surprised to learn that it was relatively easy to access the department's records, and even easier to sift through current and former employee backgrounds.

Frank Gripp stood out like a cannon among pistols, his military record as a demolitions expert the smoking gun. That, plus his very vocal antigovernment sentiment, clinched it. Scott had begun to monitor Frank's activities almost two years ago and became suspicious when Frank suddenly quit his job and isolated himself in Abel's house in Deale. When Frank's cousin showed up at the same time and they seldom left the house, Scott's investigative instincts perked up. Something smelled bad, and it wasn't the rotting fish along the Gripps' shoreline.

Taking a chance, he aimed his Nikon F6 through the window and snapped a picture.

❖

Addy stood over the grave of her grandmother, staring at the casket where it rested by the covered pit it would eventually be lowered into. On this lovely June morning, Addy had been pleased to see the turnout of neighbors who shared their memories. The priest went through the motions, but Addy only half listened. The Catholic Church had been important to her grandmother, but Addy had long since stopped attending. Still, she recited the Lord's Prayer automatically, etched into her brain through years of Catholic schooling. She had in fact taken her first communion with this priest, who had to be at least as old as her grandmother by now.

Mumbling a few Hail Marys out of consideration for her grandmother, Addy crossed herself and bent to help the aging priest from the gravesite. She was leading him to the waiting funeral home limousine when she spotted Karen standing a respectful distance away. Karen nodded, but Addy turned her head, pretending not to see her. She knew that Karen had spent more time with her family than she had over the years and had every right to be at her grandmother's funeral. But Addy didn't want to talk to her now, while she was feeling so raw and vulnerable. She wiped her eyes with her handkerchief and clung to the priest, for her own sake as much as for his.

Back at the house, Mrs. Sweetwater took charge of the arrival of huge platters of food, organizing them in the dining room and throughout the house. Meanwhile, Addy greeted familiar and not-so-familiar faces as people wandered through the rambling structure. Fern Bush, the local librarian, pushed her way to the dining room table and, with a grand flourish, displayed her pineapple upside-down cake. This presentation was received with the obligatory oohs and ahhs, and with a self-satisfied smile, Fern shoved several other plates of food out of the way to make room for the star of the show.

"Come on, now, everybody, eat up," she said. "You know, Adelaide wouldn't want to see a bunch of morose faces in her house. She'd have had you all dancing and laughing in no time."

The crowd surged to the table where the old priest liberally served up the spiked punch to these people who had known Addy's grandmother all their lives, and hers too. They were familiar to her, yet strangers after all these years, and she was distantly aware that they had been around her as she grew up, entering and exiting her life as though actors on a stage. But they were her grandmother's friends, not hers.

She left the people and smells of food and wandered to the backyard, eventually sitting in the swing that hung from an overhanging branch of the red oak.

"Caw! Caw!"

"You all right, Tommy?" she called.

"Yeah," he responded from above. "Is Grandma with the angels now?"

"Yes, yes, she is," Addy replied, more to herself than Tommy.

"What's gonna happen now?"

Addy frowned. "Well, in the morning, Grandma's lawyer is going to read her will. I guess we'll find out more then."

"And what about me?"

She barely heard Tommy's question, but the desolate sound

of his voice stabbed her heart, and she didn't know what to say. What indeed would become of them both?

"Mind if I join you?"

Addy admired Karen's casual saunter as she approached. She didn't have the energy to tell her no, or to get up and leave. Besides, Karen was the one person she knew, and she needed the company. She scooted across the seat to make room.

"Can I get you anything?" Karen asked.

Addy shook her head. "No, thanks." They swayed back and forth in the swing, listening to the sounds of the night. She felt the heat pulse from Karen's body, or was it her own? Karen's thigh barely grazed hers, yet it felt like a hot poker, branding her with Karen's mark.

"Kinda like old times, isn't it?" Karen softly observed.

"No." Addy sighed tiredly. "It's not. My grandmother is dead, I lost my job as well as my partner back in California, and I feel like I'm adrift in a storm, barely able to keep my head above water."

Karen stared at her. "Geez, Addy, I didn't know about that other stuff. I'm sorry. What are you going to do?"

Addy laughed mirthlessly. "I haven't a clue. But there's always tomorrow. I'll work something out."

"I meant what I said before. If I can do anything, you know I will. Forget about what happened. You need help now."

"I can't forget. You can't come waltzing back into my life after all this time and expect me to welcome you with a kiss. It's just not that easy."

"Why not? Dammit, Addy, we're not kids anymore."

"Because," Addy spluttered, unable to come up with a reason. She fumbled around for a few seconds more but still couldn't explain her feelings to Karen, let alone herself. Karen's mouth was slightly open, her lips moist as though she was about to speak. Her sensuous appearance distracted Addy, and she froze. She wanted to feel those lips on hers, wanted the strong arms wrapped around her as she remembered the way they felt.

Why couldn't she let instinct take over and make everything all right again?

"Because we're not kids anymore." Addy got up from the swing and ran back into the house.

Chapter Six

Addy left the attorney's office the next morning even more confused. She had hoped the will would resolve some of her problems, but it stipulated that as long as Tommy lived, the farm and the nine acres could not be sold. All hope of selling the farm to provide for Tommy's support disappeared, and Addy was in more desperate financial circumstances than she had imagined. She now needed to determine the cost of taxes, upkeep, and utilities.

She drove over to the Happy Harbor, which hadn't changed one bit. In fact, nothing about the town was different. While she had changed, everything else had remained the same, and she continued to feel strangely out of place.

Instead of entering the bar, she walked past the building to the deck in back. The Happy Harbor sat along Rockhold Creek, the charter fishing boats and pleasure craft densely packed on either side. She stood at the railing as a small fishing boat chugged into the Chesapeake, and when it finally disappeared, she walked into the restaurant. Threading her way among the tables covered with red-checkered plastic tablecloths, she entered the crowded, smoke-filled bar.

"Addy," Dee-Dee shrieked.

Addy held her arms wide open to her old friend and clung to her. Dee-Dee looked the same, although a few lines were etched in the skin around her eyes and mouth, a testament to her heavy smoking. Her long blond hair, streaked with darker shades of green and purple, hung straight down her back.

"Girl, let me see you." She held Addy at arm's length. "Wow. Fantastic. It's true what they say about California keeping you younger and healthier. Are you a vegetarian too?"

"Are you kidding?" Addy laughed. "God, it's so good to see you."

"I'm sorry about your grandmother."

"Yeah." Addy quickly sobered.

"How's Tommy taking it?"

"It's rough, on both of us, but he'll be all right. I just don't know where to go from here. I lost my job, Maureen left me, and Grandma's will says I can't sell the farm."

"Shit," Dee-Dee said. "What are you going to do?"

"I have no idea, but you know how my luck is. It can only get worse."

"Now don't start about your luck and all again." Dee-Dee poked Addy with her finger for emphasis. "Let me pour you a beer." She returned behind the counter.

"It's true, and you know it, Dee-Dee. I've had awful luck all my life, and this is just more of the continuing saga." Addy squeezed between a couple of tattooed bikers absorbed in the game on television as Dee-Dee slid a Michelob Light onto a cardboard coaster and refilled a few other empty glasses at the bar.

"So, how've you been?" Addy asked, wanting to change the subject. "What's new with you?"

"Oh, you know, same old, same old. Still working here, still single, still getting it when I can." She grinned.

"You got that right, baby," a burly biker with a red bandana wrapped around his head commented.

"Later, Blackjack," Dee-Dee said, and winked.

"Man, this place is more crowded than I remember."

"Tourist season is starting." Dee-Dee lit a cigarette and inhaled sharply. "Hey, if you need a job, I can probably get you something waitressing here."

"Thanks, but it's going to take more than that to keep the farm going. I noticed some water stains on the ceiling in the kitchen and a broken window in one of the bedrooms. The exterior needs painting and God knows what else I'll find. I have some money put away, and if I sell the house in Oakland, it'd probably be enough to make the repairs, get the place in shape, and tide me and Tommy over for a while."

Addy suddenly realized she had decided to sell the house in Oakland and was surprised at how little emotion that decision entailed. Nothing was left for her back in California. She had bought the house with the money her parents left her and never bothered to add Maureen to the title. She could do with it what she wanted.

"Well"—Dee-Dee squinted through a curlicue of smoke— "the tourists are always needing a place to stay. There ain't any hotels to speak of in the area, and a regular in here is always talking about how much money he and his wife make during the summer with their bed-and-breakfast and charter-fishing boat. I think they charge a hundred to one-fifty a night. The rich people from Annapolis and DC always want a getaway on weekends. Your place is huge. Why not turn it into a B and B?"

Addy hadn't considered the possibility, but after she quickly calculated in her head, she told Dee-Dee, "I don't think I could pull in enough money during the summer to make it viable."

Dee-Dee shrugged. "Well, then rent it year-round. Some of the locals need places to live, and we don't have much in the way of apartments either. Your house is right on the water, very nice and picturesque."

Addy let the suggestion bounce around in her brain. While she didn't particularly like the idea of being a landlord, she could put the needed funds into her coffers with very little work. It was a possible solution, anyway. "But what about Tommy? What would people think of having a grown man living in a tree house in the backyard?"

"Tommy's harmless, everyone knows that. He's been up in that tree for fifteen years and has never come down."

Addy's mind raced. If she could find a local contractor to paint the exterior, it would make a world of difference. She'd need someone to inspect the interior as well. But she still wasn't sure about the idea and wanted to talk to Tommy about it first.

❖

Either Tommy didn't fully comprehend the implications of having strangers in the house, or he didn't care. He was more absorbed in watching the inlet and seemed distracted. Addy worried that once she got her first renter, he might react differently. But she couldn't worry about that now. She had to go forward with the house repairs.

Dee-Dee recommended Dale Olson, Jeff Olson's older brother, as a contractor. She had hired him to repair both her house and the Happy Harbor. Dale had gone to high school with them, and Addy vaguely recalled a gangly, pockmarked kid. He appeared precisely the same but older, as they all were, she supposed.

"The house is structurally sound, Addy," Dale said after his inspection. "Some pipes need fixin', especially in the upstairs bathroom at the end of the hall. The kitchen could stand to be brought up to date, but that's your call. Other than that, the exterior needs some minor repairs, and a good coat of paint would definitely help."

"When can you begin?" Addy was relieved that was all he recommended.

"Pick out your paint colors and we'll get started next Monday morning."

❖

Dale showed up early that morning, a little more than a week after Addy's arrival in Deale, with Jeff in tow. Jeff was only ten years old, but with school out for the summer, he tagged along so he could hang out with Tommy. Occasionally he would help his brother on the house to earn some extra money.

While Dale and an associate installed the scaffolding, Addy drove to town to place an ad in *The Deale Picayune* about renting her rooms. She decided Dee-Dee's suggestion was at least worth a try, but if she couldn't find people she liked, she wouldn't rent to them.

"Save your money, Addy," the editor of the paper told her. "I know a couple of people wanting to rent. One of them knew your grandmother. Do you recall Fern Bush, the librarian?"

Addy winced. Everybody knew Fern Bush to be the town gossip and know-it-all. She could talk the ears off a mule and bore you to death. But Fern had known Tommy since he was a child. In fact, she had been the first to introduce him to the variety of Maryland birds, being an avian enthusiast and member of the Audubon Society. She had established Deale's local chapter and led small groups on outings along the Chesapeake. Before Tommy relegated himself to his tree house, he had been the only child to accompany the group, and he loved the excursions. For Tommy's sake, she could tolerate Fern.

"Sure, tell her to come see me, and anyone else you know. I'll at least talk with them." She was surprised at how quickly she decided to accept Fern. In no time she had gone from living in California with her girlfriend to beginning a new life in Maryland with a boarding house. She examined her emotions to see how she felt about the change, but oddly, she didn't seem to mind.

❖

Fern Bush extricated herself from her Mini Cooper and waddled to Addy's front door. The woman was in her mid-sixties and had to be nearly six feet tall and weigh three hundred pounds. She commanded any room she happened to be in, and visitors to the public library rarely talked above a whisper when she was around. Supposedly she'd buried three husbands, none of any merit save their incomes, and didn't need to work. But she had been the librarian since anyone could remember and refused to give up the power and control of her private domain.

"Good afternoon, Miss Bush." While Addy had quite naturally used the title "Ms." in California, using it in Deale, specifically with Fern Bush, would have been unthinkable. The liberated term would have offended Fern.

"Addy," Fern huffed as she climbed the steps to the porch, "I believe the risers on those steps are an inch above standard, don't you? They could wear a person out over time."

Addy restrained herself from rolling her eyes. "I'll have Dale Olson check them when he comes back tomorrow."

"Dale Olson? He's doing the work on your house? Why, that boy never so much as checked out a magazine. He doesn't have the brains of a gnat, but then, how much intelligence does it take to hold a paintbrush?"

"Dale does more than paint, Miss Bush. He's a general contractor and has to know quite a bit about a lot of things."

Fern peered at Addy as though questioning her opinion. "Hmm, we'll see, won't we?" After staring at her for a few moments, Fern placed her hands on her hips. "Well, are you going to show me inside or what?"

Addy nearly jumped. "Of course, excuse my manners. Come on in."

She showed Fern the downstairs living areas, then upstairs where most of the bedrooms were. In the large corner bedroom at the front of the house, Fern hesitated, then lumbered to the window.

"I like being able to see who's coming and going," she commented. "You can't be too safe nowadays."

Addy merely nodded. She held her breath, knowing that if the house could pass Fern's muster, anyone else would be easy to please.

Fern scanned the sunny room and ran her hand over the coverlet on the bed. The furniture was all Addy's grandmother's and emphasized the room's country décor. For a moment, Addy feared Fern would decline.

"How much did you say the rent was?"

Addy smiled. She had her first tenant.

CHAPTER SEVEN

By the end of the week, Addy had her second tenant, a retired fisherman, Chauncey Velasquez. He was originally from Mexico, where he had worked as a commercial fisherman for forty years before arriving in Deale two years ago. A short, slight man, Chauncey wore a very thin mustache and had haunted black eyes. Addy liked him because he was quiet and kept to himself. He had also taken up gardening in his retirement, offering to do what he could, and Addy was thrilled to give him full run of the grounds. In return, she cooked his meals.

At first, Fern wasn't happy that a strange man would be living in the house. But when she discovered that Chauncey loved to read about gardening, she quickly obtained him a library card, and he spent most mornings improving his knowledge while he sat in the screened-in porch. He said reading helped with his English, and Addy realized Fern liked nothing better than to educate someone. One afternoon, Fern brought Chauncey a book on topiaries, and he embraced the art form immediately, unleashing his artistic aptitude on the shrubbery.

Best of all, Tommy seemed to take the appearance of the new residents in stride. He said only that Fern looked like a seagull, her large mouth squawking all the time and her gullet constantly moving up and down. Chauncey resembled a frog—no chin and bulging eyes.

Fern, recalling Tommy's outings as a child with her Audubon group, placed birding books in his bucket and sent them up to him, delighting him with the pictures. And when Chauncey pruned dead branches and cleared a path in the tree that obscured his view of the inlet, Tommy was ecstatic. For the first time since Addy could remember, she felt as though things were going right in her life. She kept her fingers crossed.

❖

Tommy perched on the edge of his nest and tried to find stray animals in his territory. Something tan and blue caught his attention, and he stared at the bank across the inlet. The crane who had hidden in the weeds and mud behind the tractor was running along the waterline, his camera flopping around his neck. He headed straight for the water and jumped in, holding his camera up high like he was trying to keep it from getting wet. In a minute, the three men who lived in the house barreled down the hill after him. They dove into the water too, and Tommy fumbled for his binoculars to get his bird's-eye view of what was going on.

The three men were gaining on the first one, and when the crane stumbled onto the banks of Cooper property, he went down and the pelican caught up. They tumbled to the ground, arms and legs kicking and hitting. Tommy was curious about this commotion, wishing he could circle overhead and see better. The pines and tall grass were in the way, and he wondered what was going on. But if he was patient, he would know everything. He would wait until the men went away, then see what had happened.

His grandma believed he never came down from his nest, but Tommy had kept it a secret. He didn't want anyone to know he flew anywhere he wished, but only when everybody was asleep. He was a night bird and liked the quiet and freedom of the dark.

During the day, too many people were around—nosy people who poked fun at him. At night, he could be himself.

These men coming into his territory upset him. He had never seen anybody on his grandma's land except for the people she had known about. Once in a while, a fisherman on the water would pass by, trolling for smaller fish or crabbing. But this was new to him, and he stood as still as he could, waiting for the men to leave. After a while, the three men from the house walked real slow back into the water. The snipe stopped when the water was up to his knees, then turned around in Tommy's direction. For a minute, Tommy was afraid he was looking right at him, and he held his breath. But pretty soon the man continued on his way, swimming back to the other side of the inlet.

Tommy waited, wondering when the crane would come out of the tall grass. He couldn't possibly leave the area without Tommy seeing him. Either he would have to swim back across the inlet or come up onto Cooper property. Maybe he was playing down by the banks, like Tommy did at night a lot of times, hunting for signs that other creatures moved about on shore.

The longer Tommy waited, the more curious he became when the man didn't show up. A car came down the road, and Addy parked in the driveway. She was carrying some brown paper bags, groceries of some kind, and he wondered what she would bring him for his lunch. All this activity had made him hungry.

A short time later, Addy brought a tray out into the yard and placed it on the picnic table.

"I made your favorite, Tommy," she called up to the tree house. "I got the crunchy peanut butter you like, and grape jelly."

Tommy drooled. It really was his favorite meal, and he came out of his nest and stood on the platform as she put his lunch in the metal bucket, then quickly pulled it up to the landing.

"I wanted to talk to you about something," Addy said. "I saw

Grandma's lawyer again today, and everything's fine. Tomorrow will be two weeks since Grandma's funeral, and everything seems to be finalized and the house is ours. I'm going to move in and stay for good. I hope that's okay with you."

Tommy bit into his sandwich, thinking about what she said. He missed his grandma something terrible. He felt all alone, with no one to talk to. Now that Addy was back, he wasn't sure how things were going to be different. She had left him once, and she might do it again. He didn't know if he could trust her just yet, and he might have to give it some time before he was sure.

"Tommy? Is that okay with you?"

"I guess so."

"I also wanted you to know that there's going to be workmen around here for a while, doing some odd jobs but mostly painting the house. You've seen them around lately, but you may be seeing more coming and going. But mostly it will be Dale Olson, and his little brother Jeff too. I know you like Jeff. I just didn't want them to show up without you knowing about it. I didn't want you to be afraid or anything."

"Okay," he said. He didn't really like the idea of having strangers in his territory, especially after those men down by the water had been here. But having Jeff around would be fun. Maybe Jeff would help him figure out what was going on.

He took a gulp of milk and studied the tall grass and weeds where he had last seen the man in tan and blue, the crane. He still hadn't come out, and Tommy started to think something might be wrong. It kept bothering him, and he wondered if he should say something to Addy. Only he and the three men who returned to the house across the inlet knew about this secret. Surely if something wasn't right, they would have told someone.

He ate the last bite of his sandwich and finished his milk, putting the plate and glass back in the bucket and lowering it to the ground. If the man didn't come out by tonight, Tommy would go down and see what was going on.

The sun had barely sunk before Tommy climbed down the ladder and followed his usual path to the shore, keeping low to the ground. He was scared when he approached the spot where he last saw the man, but when he got there, he was surprised. He didn't see a thing. He looked real hard at the ground in front of him, with all the footprints and deep grooves in the mud leading up into the brush. Then he followed the trail where the weeds had been trampled down. Finally, he discovered something covered up about halfway by mud, grass, and a big tree limb.

CHAPTER EIGHT

After Addy finished washing the dinner dishes and put them away for the umpteenth time, she decided to get a dishwasher. Her grandmother had considered most household appliances the devil's work and refused to buy anything to make her life easier. These frivolous items cost a lot, and if they broke down, she'd need to spend even more money to have them repaired. As a result, the only modern conveniences in the house were electricity and running water, put in when Addy and her brother came to live with her. The state of Maryland insisted that she install these if she expected to remain the children's guardian.

After Grandma Adelaide added showers and toilets, she continued to expand the house. She still used the outhouse in the backyard and bathed in a wash tub filled with water she heated on the wood-burning stove, but she became enthusiastic about architecture when she realized what fun construction work could be. She did much of the work herself, learning from books she borrowed from the library. It was hard, physical labor, the kind her grandmother was used to and loved. By the time of her death, she had added four bedrooms, three bathrooms, and a family room. And when Tommy decided to stay in the tree house permanently, she ran plumbing, heating, and electricity up the old oak and installed insulation. She expanded his small room and added a tiny kitchenette and bathroom.

Addy dried her hands on the dish towel and stood at the kitchen sink, gazing out into the night to see if Tommy was okay. Things were going well, with the new tenants and the house already in much better condition. She needed to get her real estate in Oakland on the market and determined to call her realtor in California the next morning. Right now, she hoped her savings and the income from the tenants would be enough for them until the house sold. She considered hunting for another job, but the town was small and businesses scarce, so she knew salaries would be low. Perhaps doing people's taxes might help, but tax season was a long way off. She couldn't leave Tommy alone all day anyway—someone needed be around to fix his meals and keep an eye on him. Fern still worked, and Addy didn't feel right about asking Chauncey.

Staring out the window again, she wondered if Tommy was awake. It was still early. Maybe she should spend some time with him. She wanted to be sure all the changes in his life weren't too much of a strain, and besides, she was a little lonely. She tossed the dish towel onto the counter and wandered out the back door.

"Tommy? Tommy, are you awake?"

Not waiting for a response, she climbed the oak and scrambled to the door, knocking briefly before she went inside.

"Tommy?" She groped in the dark until she found the switch to Tommy's bedside lamp. His bed was empty and Tommy nowhere in sight.

"Tommy, where are you?"

She began to shake and she panicked, thinking something bad had happened to him. Maybe she should call the police. That meant calling Karen, and while her body instantly perked up, her mind rebelled. She forced herself to calm down and think clearly.

She didn't see any signs of distress in the room. In fact, Tommy's bed was neatly made. Could he have voluntarily left his tree house? He never went down, but then, who would pay any attention to him at night when everyone was in bed? She rushed to the window with its open shutters. The half-moon reflecting off the water provided enough light for her to see, and she squinted into the darkness. After a few moments, she detected movement down by the water, and she ran to the platform and stumbled down the ladder.

She sprinted to the pine trees and into the tall grass dotting the inlet banks, at one point tripping and falling to her knees in the mud. Pausing only for an instant, she scrambled to her feet and trod more carefully near the water's edge.

"Tommy? Tommy, where are you?" *Please, oh, please, God. Where is he?* Tommy was her baby brother, whom she had held in her arms as a little girl, if for only a few moments. She had loved him like a favorite doll then, and as they grew older he became her best friend and confidant. When they lost their parents, they had had only one another, and they had defended each other.

"Caw, caw! Over here, Addy."

His voice washed over her so rapidly that her knees nearly gave out. Stepping cautiously into the weedy grass, she reached an opening where the ground had been trampled and found Tommy standing next to a mound of dirt, a large branch in his hands. She rushed to his side and wrapped her arms around him.

"Thank God you're all right. What in the world are you doing out here? Are you okay?" Her words tumbled out, and she breathed deeply to calm herself. Her sudden release of tension made it difficult to stand.

"I could kill you, Tommy. Don't ever do this again without telling me. It's dangerous. You could drown and I'd never know it. What are you doing out here in the dark?"

Tommy pointed to the mound of dirt. "He's dead, just like Grandma."

Confused, Addy stared at the pile of earth.

"What? Who's dead? What are you talking about?"

"The man with the camera. He was playing hide-and-seek,

but he's not very good at it. And look, he's dead just like Grandma. Do you think he's with the angels now too, Addy?"

The night sky and bright moon created a surreal landscape, as though Addy were dreaming or moving through water. She tripped over something—a pair of feet sticking out from the mud. She pressed a fist to her mouth, suppressing the scream and bile that rushed to her throat. Unable to comprehend the horrific scene before her, she stared at Tommy instead, and for the longest time, she tried to process exactly what was going on. He held the branch in his hands, as if he had either clubbed the man with it or was using it to cover up the body.

"Tommy...what...what are you doing?"

He grinned, his teeth gleaming even in the darkness.

"I'm burying him. I tried covering up his head better. It was kind of bashed in, so I put more mud on it. I was going to put some grass on his legs so all of him would be buried—just like Grandma. But I scratched myself on this limb. I think I got a splinter in my hand too. Can you get it out, Addy?"

He held up his hand and she automatically moved closer. Holding it, she stared at his palm, unseeing, so she shook her head to clear it. Everything was happening so suddenly, and she couldn't quite grasp what was going on and what Tommy's role in it was. She felt numb yet shivered violently in the warm summer air.

Kneeling beside the body, she felt hopefully for a pulse, but found none.

"Tommy, let's go back to the house so I can take care of your hand."

"But what about him? I need to finish burying him."

"Not tonight. Come on, Tommy. I need to think about this."

Taking his arm, she dragged him along, half leaning on him for support. She started to take him into the house, but he pulled back, insisting on returning to his tree house. She nodded dully, and after getting some first-aid cream, tweezers, and a bandage, she followed him. He sat on his bed, staring at his hands, the bedside lamp shining brightly like a beacon in the darkness.

Sitting next to him, she said, "Let me see."

His hands were covered in blood, much more than a simple sliver of wood could ever produce. Her heart stopped beating and she couldn't move.

"Oh, Tommy. What did you do?"

"I got a splinter when I accidentally dropped the club on the man. I didn't mean to, Addy. Is my hand going to be okay?"

Addy couldn't keep from shaking. She held on to Tommy's hands, unable to let go of them. Finally, she got up and poured a bowl full of water from the pitcher on the table. Grabbing a towel, she began to wash his hands. The water in the bowl turned bright red, and she scrubbed his hands roughly, trying to rid him of the stain.

"Ow! Addy, you're hurting me."

"I'm sorry." She stilled her hands. Finding a small sliver in his thumb, she removed it with the tweezers, then applied the medication and bandage. "Tommy, listen to me very carefully. You need to stay here in your tree house. Don't leave it for a while, because I don't want you to get your hands dirty. You could get a bad infection. And if anyone asks you about the man down by the water, don't say anything. Even if it's the police, say that you don't know anything about the man. You never saw him before, okay?"

"But if Karen asks, it's okay then, right? She's my friend. And Jeff Olson, he's my friend too."

Addy shook her head. "No. Promise you won't say a word to anyone and that you'll stay right here. I mean it, Tommy. This is very important. Say it."

"I promise."

"Now, go to sleep, and don't climb down again tonight. Good night, Tommy." She kissed his forehead and left him sitting on his bed.

Back in the house, she sat down at the kitchen table, shaking uncontrollably. What should she do? Perhaps call Karen, tell her everything and that Tommy couldn't be held accountable for his actions. He didn't even understand most of what he did. Hell, he thought he was a bird, had believed it since he was a boy. After his parents disappeared, he had climbed up into the tree house and never budged—at least that's what everyone believed. But he did indeed come down, and for what purposes she could only guess!

She glimpsed her nearby cell phone. She should call Karen. She'd know what to do. Just thinking of Karen here in the room, with her quiet strength, taking charge of the situation, as she had so many times in the past, calmed her. Karen had been with her when Addy had found out about her parents, and even though they were just children, she seemed to know how to make things right.

And Karen had been her first love, leading her gently into the unknown world of self-discovery. She had shielded Addy against the people shocked by their relationship and defended Tommy from the taunts and fists of other boys. Karen was her champion, like those she read about in fairy tales, and she had believed in her without question.

In that instant, she almost reached for the phone. But she was exhausted and still needed to mentally process the evening's events. What would happen to Tommy if he were arrested and convicted of murder? He would never survive. Addy had to defend him from the real world. Maybe she would be able to think more clearly in the morning. After that, she would call Karen.

Chapter Nine

The sound of tires crunching on the stones in the driveway roused Addy from a deep sleep. She had awakened several times during the night, restless with her secret. Her dreams had been anxious too, with snippets of visions—the inlet, the shoreline, the body, and Tommy's bloody hands. The thunderstorm hadn't helped. The rain cascaded down, obscuring her view of the inlet.

Hearing a car door slam, she crawled out of bed and hurried to the window, her mind instantly on alert. Karen was getting out of the patrol car, fresh and crisp in her uniform. Addy's heart thumped painfully, from either relief or anxiety, but she was still glad to see her.

She threw on her bathrobe and flew down the stairs, intercepting Karen before she could knock.

"Mornin', Addy. Sorry to bother you so early."

"No, it's all right, come on in. Let me make some coffee." Addy hustled into the kitchen, too nervous to ask why she was here. Could someone have discovered the body already and even now the police were on their way? Was Karen here to ease the way for the arresting officers to haul Tommy off to jail? Opening the canister of coffee, Addy spilled half the contents on the floor.

"Hey, are you all right?" Karen knelt and began to scoop the coffee with her hand. Glancing up, she stared at Addy. "You're pale. Are you sick?"

"No, no, I'm fine. I just didn't sleep well last night." She bent to help with the cleanup. Oh, how she wanted to fall into Karen's arms. She wanted to be held and told that everything would be all right. She inhaled Karen's scent, nothing but soap and clean skin, and warm memories crept into her already muddled brain. It felt so good to have Karen in the house again. But now what would happen? "What are you doing here?"

"I was hanging out at the Happy Harbor last night when Dee-Dee mentioned you were turning the place into a boarding house."

"Oh, that." Addy laughed nervously.

"She said you have two tenants, including old lady Bush. Geez, what a nightmare that must be."

"Why, good morning, *Deputy*."

Fern entered the kitchen, dressed in seersucker and ready for a day at work.

"Oh, uh, good morning, Miss Bush. I didn't see you come in." Karen blushed.

"Evidently. As I recall, you were equally unobservant as a child. I believe you rarely borrowed a book and when you did, well, let me just say that your taste in literature was questionable."

"How do you remember that stuff?" Karen asked, surprise plastered across her face.

"I never forget anything, Deputy. Knowledge sharpens the mind. It's obvious you haven't picked up a book since then."

"I went into the military after high school, remember, Miss Bush?" Karen asked. "The officers there sharpened my mind plenty."

Fern sniffed and scrutinized Karen. "I'm sure that was precisely the correct fit for someone of your…talents. Now, Addy here, she went off to a prestigious university and made something of herself. I'm sure she's as keen as a razor."

"Huh?" The heat rose to Addy's face, and Karen's scrutiny did nothing to turn it down. Fern poured coffee into a thermos and left for work. They were silent for a long while and Addy didn't know what to say, though images from last night flooded her. Tommy simply couldn't hurt any living creature. Surely he hadn't acted intentionally. It had to have been an accident. That's it. That's what she would tell the police.

But why would he have tried to bury the man's body? What excuse would she possibly concoct, other than that she had been an accomplice and tried to cover up the crime? *Oh, man, this is getting more complicated than I thought.*

"Addy, are you all right?"

"I need to talk to you—"

A shout drew their attention to the backyard. Addy ran out to the screened-in porch to see a small boat moored alongside the dock. Two men, standing near the shore, waved frantically, motioning them down to the water. A heavy lump dropped into her stomach and she felt like she was swallowing sand. Karen hurried out of the porch and into the yard, heading for the men and Addy rushed after her.

"Karen, wait!"

Karen stopped midstride and slowly turned around. It was the first time Addy had called her by her first name, and she shivered slightly. Addy had been acting strangely ever since she arrived. And now Addy seemed terrified. She almost reached out, but stopped herself, knowing she wouldn't be welcome. Something wasn't right, and she wanted very much to erase Addy's fear, but she would have to make the first move.

"What is it?"

"I…I," Addy stuttered. "I just wanted to say be careful. You don't know who those men are or what they want."

Karen gazed at her for a long time. Did Addy really care for her safety or did she have something else on her mind?

She resumed walking toward the water. "Actually, I do know

those men. They're locals, two retired guys who go out fishing most mornings. They're okay."

They stumbled along the water's edge, their feet bogging more than once in the mud, made deeper by the previous evening's downpour.

A tall, white-haired man dressed in L.L.Bean fishing attire pointed to the ground. "Hey, Deputy. Come quick. Look what we found."

Karen squatted in the mud. At first she believed the rains had uncovered the body. She wanted to vomit but immediately suppressed the urge because of the onlookers. She had seen dead bodies before, especially in the army, but had never grown immune to the experience.

"Someone bashed his brains in," the shorter man said.

Addy was overcome with nausea. While it was true, hearing it spoken aloud in such a crude fashion sickened her. She turned her head away from the battered form. It was too late now—too late to tell Karen what she knew. Karen would wonder why she hadn't called her last night, as soon as she found Tommy standing over the body, his hands dripping with blood. How had everything gone wrong so quickly?

"I need to call the station." Karen straightened up with mud on the hem of her pants in addition to the back of her pant legs, already splattered with brown spots kicked up from her boot heels. Pointing to the men, she said, "You two stay here. I'll need to take your statements. Addy, come with me."

Karen stomped off through the mud and Addy followed her docilely. *She knows. Or at least she suspects.* What would she tell her? Yes, she'd come out last night hunting for Tommy, who never ventured out of the tree, only to find him standing over the body? And then she'd kept it a secret? God, she and Tommy were *both* going to wind up in prison.

As they approached the house, Addy chanced a look up at the tree house. Tommy stared down at her, his face expressionless.

She didn't know if he fully comprehended his actions, but if necessary, she would get an attorney to plead he was mentally incompetent to stand trial. Even so, they'd want to commit him to some type of institution, and she couldn't allow that to happen either. She held her finger up to her lips and he nodded.

They entered the house through the kitchen and Karen told her to stay put while she went out to the patrol car to call in the crime. As she sat at the kitchen table waiting for Karen to return, she fidgeted with the salt and pepper shakers. *Oh, God.* If she'd only said something sooner.

❖

Frank stood at the window and trained his binoculars on the police as they wrapped wide yellow tape around a pine tree. Eventually they'd get around to visiting their house, asking if they had seen anything unusual. *No, Officer, we were watching the game and didn't see a thing.*

"Now what are they doing, Frank?" Abel asked as he lit a cigarette.

"Well, by now they're probably hunting clues, anything that can help identify the body and who killed him. Luckily it rained last night and washed away footprints."

"Yeah, it's a good thing," Clarence said.

"Shut up, you idiot. If you'd been keeping an eye out like you were supposed to, that reporter would never have been able to spy on us." Frank drew a wallet out of his pocket, examining the contents. "He was only a local reporter. If he was worth his salt, he'd have been working for the big league. I don't think we have anything to worry about."

He tossed the wallet into the trash bin. He would personally burn it in the barrel after the police left so he didn't draw suspicion to the house. With this last piece of evidence gone, they should escape detection. Things might be hot for a while and they would have to lay low. But the cops would soon lose interest when they couldn't solve the crime. They would gradually stop coming every day, and Frank could return to his task. He wasn't in a hurry, but he was destined to make a name for himself—if not by being a war hero, then by getting back at the federal government.

❖

The police were crawling around the property like little ants hurrying to gather food. Tommy supposed the activity had something to do with the man he had found down by the water, but he guessed Addy would fill him in later.

He was glad Karen was there to help. He liked Karen. After Jeff Olson, she was his next best friend, and that was only because she was a girl. Addy was a girl too, and she was his sister, but Tommy wasn't so sure she was as good a friend as Jeff and Karen. It was nice to know that she would be living in the house, though, kind of like the way things used to be. He was happy then and wished things had never changed.

He sighed, got down on his hands and knees, and crawled under his bed. Pulling a nylon duffel bag out from underneath it, he unzipped it to reveal all the treasures he had found or been given over the years. Ignoring most of the contents, he dug around until he found what he wanted—that man's camera with the letters N-I-K-O-N on the front. After Addy thought he was asleep last night, he had gone back to where the man was and picked it up. The word on it was funny, not like anything he'd ever seen, but he understood what a camera was. He held it up and saw his table through the viewfinder. He didn't know how to make it work, though. Maybe Karen would show him.

Karen had taught him how to do a lot of things, like whittle with his jackknife so that twigs looked like birds. Or how to rub two sticks together on a pile of dry leaves and start a fire. That was cool, but it was really hard. Tommy practiced, but still wasn't very good at it.

Maybe tomorrow, when all the other policemen weren't around, he'd ask her to come up and teach him how to make the camera work.

Chapter Ten

As Liberty waited for her luggage at BWI, she scrutinized everyone in the claim area for signs of anything unusual. Satisfied nothing was amiss, she gathered her bags and headed for the rental-car agency. A blast of heat and humidity assaulted her when the automatic doors slid open. After spending two weeks wrapping up her last case in the milder climate of the Midwest, she noticed the contrast immediately. It promised to be a typical Fourth of July weekend in a few days, and she wiped her brow at the idea. Before retrieving her car, she got a map and directions to a small town called Deale on the Chesapeake.

The file she'd received about the new case contained reports from various scientists and their assessment of water samples from the area around Deale. These scientists, collaborating with the FBI, were also members of Infragard. Liberty had begun with the FBI as an IT analyst when Infragard's sole interest had been to monitor cyberspace. But 9/11 changed all that. Her passion for environmental issues had led her to become involved in the National Infrastructure Protection Center under the auspices of Homeland Security.

As she headed down the Parkway on her way to Deale, her cell phone rang—"Girls Just Want to Have Fun"—and she flipped it open.

"Liberty."

"You're to meet the Deale sheriff when you get there. He's assigned a deputy to work with you." Her handler always dispensed with the niceties and got straight to the point. "They'll be the only ones who know your real identity. Otherwise your cover is the same."

Liberty was proud of her national, and international, reputation as an environmental activist. She never had to pretend, though, that she cared about the water she drank, the air she breathed, or the animals that inhabited the earth. She believed in the well-being of the planet with all that was in her. It just happened to be a convenient cover for her work with the FBI.

"Additional agents are on the way to investigate the possible terrorism angle, but they've been told about you, why you're there, and the work you'll be doing with local law enforcement."

"Is the deputy any good?"

"She's a member of Infragard, so she knows the routine, and I personally read her file. Former Army Intelligence from a family of army officers. She checks out."

"Okay. I'll call you with an update after I get there and settle in."

"Anything you want me to tell the sheriff?"

"Tell him not to worry. I'm on my way." She flipped the cell phone off, merged onto Interstate 97, and headed south. Having to deal with small-town police made her sigh. They were usually more of a hindrance than a help, but they were necessary in handling the paperwork, a task she loathed.

❖

Addy sat at the kitchen table, exhausted by the day's events. Several detectives, including Karen, had questioned her, and while she denied seeing or hearing anything, she felt guilty. Karen had eyed her suspiciously, seeming not to believe a word she said. So Addy declared her innocence more loudly and vehemently and became even more certain that Karen saw through her.

Having Karen in the room, witnessing her interview, comforted yet unsettled her. The heat of Karen's stare burned a hole through her heart, and she wished she could confess everything to her. But what would they do to Tommy? He couldn't survive confinement, but, if he had done this, could he do it again? Could she be certain he was responsible? Why had she ever left Maryland in the first place? Tommy was as much her responsibility as her grandmother's, perhaps more so. She had failed him, but she would make up for it now. She would fight for him like a mother defending her young.

The police also questioned Fern and Chauncey, separately, so Addy didn't know the outcome. Shortly afterward, Chauncey had left, appearing shaken by the encounter. Hopefully she wouldn't lose them as renters. A murder on her property would definitely dampen any prospect of future tenants. The police were familiar with Tommy's strange behavior. Some knew him, and Karen had filled in the others. So when someone suggested that they question him, Addy held her breath. Fortunately Karen had dissuaded them from wasting their time.

Despite her fatigue, she rose and walked into the backyard. Seeing a light up in the tree, she climbed the ladder and knocked.

"You're still up?" she asked Tommy.

"It was fun seeing all the police. Are they coming back tomorrow?"

"I don't know, maybe." She tried to catch any sign of guilt in him. Did he feel remorse? Was he capable of such complex emotions?

"Tommy, I need to talk to you about the man you were burying last night."

"Okay. I'm sorry if I didn't do a good job. Were the police mad?"

Addy's chest constricted painfully, and her throat was so tight she could barely speak. She struggled to phrase her questions so she could elicit coherent comments from him without alarming him.

"The police are sad because the man is dead. Do you understand, Tommy? It's like when Grandma died. It made you sad, right?"

Tommy vigorously nodded.

"Well, they only want to know what happened. How he died. They want to understand so they can stop it from happening to someone else."

She searched his face, seeking comprehension. When he sat quietly, waiting for her to continue, she decided to plunge in.

"Tommy, do you know how the man died?"

Tommy's face scrunched up in concentration, but after a few moments, he shook his head. Addy sighed and tried another tack. Tommy spent entire days staring out at the inlet and the shoreline around it. Surely he'd seen something. He'd made a strange comment last night, but she couldn't recall what it was.

"Tommy, everyone thinks you stay up here in your tree and never come down. I did too. But last night you came down. Do you do that all the time?"

"Sometimes. It's safe at night and nobody makes fun of me." He hesitated, looking sheepish. "Are you mad at me, Addy?"

Addy could barely control her tears. Not knowing why she even bothered to keep them hidden, she threw her arms around Tommy's neck and let them flow freely.

"No, Tommy, I'm not mad at you. I love you very much and never want to hurt you." She clung to him so long that he finally begged her to let him go. After tucking him in, she wearily climbed down the tree and went to her room. She didn't sleep, but paced most of the night. She needed to make a decision about her brother in the morning and prayed it would be the right one.

❖

Karen sat at the bar in the Happy Harbor, nursing a cup of coffee as Dee-Dee worked. It was late, and the knot in her gut told her something wasn't right. It was Addy. Finding a dead body on her property had clearly upset her, and the officers who questioned her probably hadn't helped.

But she suspected something more in Addy's distress. Her cop's instincts had flickered on, as they did when she approached the scene of a crime, and her senses were on high alert. Addy had reacted oddly to the murder, not like a normal person would. She had been defensive. Karen had known Addy all her life and sensed immediately that she wasn't being forthcoming.

She swiveled on her bar stool when the door opened and a strikingly handsome woman entered the bar. She had to be a stranger, probably a tourist, because Karen would have definitely noted the competition. Dee-Dee's attention had also been drawn to the door, and she went through her pre-mating ritual—a toss of her color-streaked hair, a slow, easy grin, and a bit of swagger as she crossed to the other side of the bar.

"Well, hey there, handsome," Dee-Dee drawled. "What's your pleasure?"

"Fresh-squeezed carrot juice, if you have it." The newcomer sat next to Karen at the bar.

"Huh?" Dee-Dee asked.

"Bottled water." The woman's gaze met Karen's. "Good evening, Deputy."

"Evenin'," Karen responded. "New in town?"

"Yes, just got in." She opened the bottled water and took a long swallow. Returning it to the counter, she waved her hand back and forth in front of her face. "Uh, aren't there any no-smoking bans in Maryland?"

"Only in the restaurant in back. The bars are still considered smoking areas." Dee-Dee quickly stashed her pack of Kools under the bar.

"Maybe you can help me, Deputy. I may be spending some

time in Deale and I need a place to stay. I've checked in to a hotel outside of town, but I'd like something closer. Any ideas?"

Dee-Dee jumped in. "My friend, Addy Cooper, has a huge house on the water. It's got a boat dock and several acres of wooded land, very private and quiet."

Karen tried to signal Dee-Dee to stop, but she was too intent on serving up her breasts on the counter in front of the stranger. Her strategically opened blouse exposed more than it covered, and the stranger gazed hungrily at the display.

"Addy Cooper?" she asked. "The place sounds perfect. If you wouldn't mind giving me directions, I'll call on her in the morning."

Karen scowled at Dee-Dee, who raised a questioning eyebrow. If Dee-Dee wanted to pounce on any creature that happened into her bar, that was up to her. But pointing the woman in Addy's direction, particularly now that she was back in town and single, might throw a monkey wrench into Karen's plans at reconciliation.

"I'd be happy to take you there myself in the morning, if you like," Dee-Dee offered. Her breasts rolled dangerously close to knocking the bottled water over. "Addy's my best friend."

"Well, I wouldn't want to put you out." The stranger's gaze became a stare.

"Oh, I don't mind putting out—I mean being put out," Dee-Dee said, and giggled girlishly.

Karen thought she would puke. She would have to keep an eye on this stranger. She didn't like the way the woman glibly chatted with Dee-Dee, her eyes rarely leaving the bartender's chest. Granted, Dee-Dee had a nice pair, but this stranger had a confidence and wolfishness about her Karen didn't appreciate. She was cocky, and Karen wanted her to know who the local stud was.

"So, you didn't say what your business was in town." Karen was glad to interrupt the love fest going on in front of her.

The woman stopped laughing and glared at her. "No, I

didn't." She returned to her conversation with Dee-Dee, who handed her another bottle of water, on the house.

That did it. Karen definitely didn't like the stranger. Who cared that she was good-looking and dressed in jeans that hugged her like a woman. She could have Dee-Dee if she wanted, but she better damn well stay away from Addy.

CHAPTER ELEVEN

Karen dragged herself into the station the next morning, still bleary-eyed from one too many after she got home from the Happy Harbor. That, and a restless night dreaming of Addy, left her tired and grumpy. She poured herself the dregs of coffee still left from the night shift and plopped down at her desk.

Just before she finished her morning ritual and started on patrol, the chief called her into his office, which was never a good sign, so she entered warily. She froze, then recoiled. The stranger from the bar was sitting in front of the chief's desk. "Officer Kaczarowski, meet Special Agent Liberty McDonald. Agent, this is your InfraGard associate."

Karen tried to appear as blasé as possible, but the agent with the smart-ass grin had to know she'd surprised her. The well-known environmental activist had once spent nearly a year living in a huge redwood tree that a logging company wanted to chainsaw to death. She was a leader in the fight to save old-growth forests and had won despite corporate greed.

"Agent." Karen nodded, but didn't offer her hand.

"Officer Kaz, Kazro, uh, a pleasure to see you, again."

"You two know each other?" the chief asked.

"We met last night at the Happy Harbor, but the agent didn't identify herself." Karen wanted to punch the grin off her face but instead sat in the other chair opposite the desk. "So what's going on, Agent McDonald?"

"Please, call me Liberty. Here's a copy of the reports I have so far." She handed Karen a thick dossier.

"You can read them later, but basically they say top scientists from the EPA have been examining samples from the waters around Deale and have discovered increasing levels of radioactivity. Since there is no known source, we are treating this as a possible terrorist threat. While not yet a danger to humans, it is causing dead fish to wash ashore, and we're beginning to see collateral damage to other life forms and the surrounding wetlands."

"Do you have any suspects?" Karen asked.

"Not yet. My only possible lead is from a local newspaper reporter. The guy's name is"—Liberty flipped through a few pages of her notepad—"Scott Vinson."

Karen glanced at her boss, who stared gravely back at her.

"What is it?" Liberty asked.

"Scott Vinson was found dead yesterday morning. The editor of the paper where he worked identified the body."

Surprise flashed across the agent's face and just as quickly faded away. She leaned forward. "What have you got?"

"Not much so far," the chief admitted. "The autopsy showed that it wasn't a blow to the head that caused death, as we suspected at first. Someone impaled the poor bastard with a sharp branch. It's in the lab for analysis."

"Other evidence?" Liberty wrote as the chief spoke.

"Unfortunately, it rained the night before the body was found. That and the incoming tide washed away any footprints in the area. The body was intact and partially submerged in mud and water, but it hadn't been there long. His editor said he'd talked to him just that morning and Vinson said he was working on a big story. When the editor asked him about it, he only said it had to do with something going on down by the inlet. And that's where we found him."

"Can you show me where you found the body, Officer Kaz, Kazro—?"

"Call me Karen," she snapped. "I assume you're on your way there already. That is, if you still plan to rent a room from Addy Cooper?"

"The body was found on her property? Interesting." Liberty stroked her chin.

"Not so interesting." Karen didn't want her to jump to the wrong conclusion. "The body was found there, but I think we can safely rule out the Coopers. The woman and her brother aren't the type and have no criminal record."

"Still, I'd like to check them out." Liberty rose from her chair.

"I'll drive you over," Karen said.

"No. I'm operating undercover, so that would only draw suspicion. Besides, the lovely bartender made me a kind offer, remember? I'll be renting a room at the Coopers' after all."

The agent thanked the chief and swaggered out the station door. Karen really didn't like that woman. And the possibility that she might be moving in on Addy didn't appeal to her either.

❖

Addy sat in a lawn chair under the red oak, staring up at the tree house. What should she do? If only she had someone to confide in. She simply couldn't make this decision about her brother alone. Several times she had reached for the phone to call Karen, and then she lost her nerve. The criminal justice system would destroy Tommy. He knew nothing about the real world, let alone prison or a mental institution. How she wished Grandma Adelaide was still alive. She had known what to do in every situation. Would Addy ever be as capable and strong as her grandmother?

Suddenly she had an idea and, determined to get at the truth, she climbed the tree.

When he let her in, she sat him down at the little table in his room and poured them both a glass of water. "Tommy, I need to talk to you. We need to talk about the man you were trying to bury, okay?"

Tommy stared warily at her, but nodded.

"Why did you hit the man with the stick, Tommy? Was he doing something bad to you?"

Tommy slowly shook his head.

"Then why, Tommy? Why did you hit him?"

"It was an *accident*, Addy. I told you."

"I know, sweetie, but I also know you wouldn't hurt anybody. Have you ever hurt anyone before?"

"No."

"See," Addy said, relieved to hear this wasn't a habit. "So that's why I wonder why you would do it now. Did he *say* something you didn't like?"

"No, he was just lying there."

"Lying there?" Addy was confused. "You mean, after you hit him?"

"No, I found him that way. I accidentally dropped the stick on him when I was trying to bury him."

A wave of relief so great washed over her that she began to cry. Tommy hadn't killed the reporter, he'd found him already dead.

"Did I do something wrong, Addy?"

"No, sweetie, no," she said, and hugged him. "No, you're a good boy and you didn't do anything wrong."

He was clearly telling the truth, that he hadn't killed the reporter. But who had? If the police learned Tommy had discovered the body and tried to cover it, they'd never believe him.

Addy heard a car and glimpsed a Ford pickup barreling down the road. As it drew closer, she could see Dee-Dee behind the wheel and someone she couldn't make out in the passenger seat. When the truck disappeared behind the front of the house, she stepped out onto the decking.

"We'll talk more about this later, Tommy. Don't worry, but we still need to keep this a secret, just between you and me. Remember?"

"I can remember, Addy. No credit, and no talking about the man."

His innocent expression tore at her heart as she climbed down the ladder.

"I'm so glad to see you," Addy called as Dee-Dee walked up the driveway.

"I've brought you another renter," Dee-Dee said, her face practically glowing.

Dee-Dee's companion sauntered casually to the house, and her long legs and dark eyes made Addy's heart dance a jig. She hadn't seen anyone that handsome since, well, since Karen. When the woman's burning gaze met hers, she felt it to her toes.

"Liberty McDonald," she said, extending her hand.

"Liberty. I'm Addy Cooper, and this is my house." She waved an all-encompassing arm behind her.

"Dee-Dee was right. It certainly is huge. And you have two other renters?"

"Fern Bush and Chauncey Velasquez. I'll introduce them to you, if you like. Come on in."

She showed her around the house while Dee-Dee followed like a puppy. Of all the large bedrooms available, Liberty seemed most drawn to one at the back.

"Well, the view of the water is nice," Addy acknowledged, "but the room is a bit small. I could charge you less—"

"I wouldn't think of it. Besides, all I plan to do in this room is sleep. I spend most of my time outdoors."

"I can tell," Dee-Dee said. "You're in great shape. And all you really need is a full-size bed. Even a twin will do in a pinch." She sat on the bed and bounced up and down.

Addy stared. Something was going on between Dee-Dee and her friend. "So, how long have you known each other?"

"Oh, we just met last night at the bar, but it feels like I've known her forever," Dee-Dee gushed, slipping her hand into the crook of Liberty's arm.

"I see." Addy suppressed a grin. Liberty was about to become another notch in Dee-Dee's bedpost. She wondered why that bothered her.

"Could I check out the grounds?" Liberty asked.

"Oh, uh, sure. Right this way."

Addy led them through the kitchen to the screened-in porch and out into the backyard. The breeze coming off the water brought with it the scent of salt and loam, and Addy inhaled it deeply. The smells recalled her childhood, and a wave of nostalgia enveloped her. While Liberty strolled down to the dock, she glanced up at the tree house.

"Does she know about Tommy?"

"I mentioned him on the way over," Dee-Dee replied. "My God, she has a great ass, doesn't she?"

"Uh-huh." Addy shook herself from her admiration of the woman's backside. "I mean, she is handsome, in an androgynous sort of way. If you like them that way."

"She looks a lot like Karen," Dee-Dee said, turning to Addy. "I thought *you* liked them that way."

Addy shook her head. "Not anymore."

As the newcomer stood on the dock and stared out across the water, Addy dared admit to herself that she was indeed attracted to Liberty. But she had enough problems on her hands without inviting that kind of trouble into her life.

❖

"So, you and Addy are best friends?" Liberty asked as Dee-Dee drove them back to town.

"Yes, well, sort of."

"Sort of?" Liberty scanned Dee-Dee's breasts, wondering how they'd feel in her hands.

"Well, I knew her in high school, but she went off to college six years ago. Addy moved back to town over two weeks ago, after her grandmother got creamed by a dishwasher-sized piece of space junk. She inherited the house and of course the responsibility of caring for Tommy."

"Of course. He's a nutcase, isn't he?" Liberty wondered how much Dee-Dee knew.

"Tommy? Oh, he's a doll. He just wasn't able to adapt to the loss of his parents when he was a kid, and now he's lost his grandmother. It's been rough on him. That's how he copes with things."

"You don't think he's a danger to himself? Or others?"

Dee-Dee glanced sideways at her. "Tommy? He wouldn't hurt a flea. Besides, he never comes down out of that tree and no one goes up, except one or two people he trusts. If you're worried about him, don't be. He's a good kid once you get to know him."

"I'm sure he is."

Liberty fully intended to get to know him, and his very attractive sister. But in the meantime, Dee-Dee had made it clear that she was expecting a good time. And Liberty planned to give it to her. This country bumpkin would probably appreciate someone with her sexual prowess, and Liberty was definitely in the mood. It had been weeks since she'd had sex.

Dee-Dee's right hand dropped off the steering wheel and landed on Liberty's thigh, her thumb rubbing circles on her leg. The tingling sensation flooded her body and she leaned back, enjoying the seduction. This would be easier than she had imagined. Dee-Dee was a bartender and, from all appearances, was friendly with the clientele in more ways than one.

Addy was an entirely different animal. She would want to be wooed—wined and dined, and all that. Liberty wondered what kind of decent food and wine she could find out here in the backwoods. But she liked a challenge every now and again. And Addy was definitely worth the wait. Her slender figure, full breasts, and chocolate brown hair made for a very enticing package.

Dee-Dee's hand traveled up the inside of Liberty's leg and found the seam at her crotch. Her fingernails teased and scratched, and Liberty's body went on full alert. Oh, yeah, this was going to be a lot of fun.

CHAPTER TWELVE

Liberty moved in the next day with surprisingly few possessions. Addy wondered exactly what she did for a living, but when Liberty paid the first three months' rent in cash, she figured what Liberty did was none of her business. She prepared a roast for dinner that night so all her tenants could get to know one another, and hoped Liberty would divulge more of her background then. Since it was a warm evening, she lit candles out on the porch to make the occasion more festive.

"Where are you from originally, Liberty?" Fern asked as she served up a mountain of mashed potatoes.

"Johnsonville, in upstate New York, but I travel so much now, I don't really have a place to call home. You?"

Fern jerked her head up, obviously startled. Addy had to hide her smile behind her napkin. Fern wasn't used to being on the receiving end of questions.

"Why, I was born and raised right here. I wouldn't dream of living anywhere else. Why do you travel so much? What do you do for a living that you haven't settled down in one place?"

"Oh, I'm fortunate to work protecting our environment. I'm here doing some studies on the Chesapeake."

"Aha. Well, whatever you need to know, I can help you there." Fern scooped up a forkful of salad and examined it intently. "I've read quite a bit on the subject, from nutrient pollutants to sedimentation, air, and toxic pollutants. What's happening to our beautiful bay is a disgrace."

"I agree. What about you, Mr. Velasquez?"

Chauncey stopped chewing, his fork frozen in midair. "Me?"

"Yes. What do you think? You've been a fisherman on these waters. You've probably seen some change—the decline in the blue crab population that Maryland is known for, the effects of pollution on the coastline, and so on."

"*Sí*, yes, that is true."

"And where are you from originally?" Liberty pressed him. "I hear an accent there. Puerto Rico?"

"Mexico." Chauncey put his fork on his plate and glanced down at his lap, then at the door. He was acting curious, like he might bolt from the room, which was unusual for him.

"Caw! Caw!"

"I'm sorry. I must see to my brother." Addy was mortified by Tommy's behavior in her new boarder's presence.

When she reached the backyard, the sound of exploding firecrackers and rockets in the distance startled her. She recalled watching the fireworks displays over San Francisco Bay with Maureen, and a twinge of sadness enveloped her. Tommy stuck his head out the window.

"Could I have some more mashed potatoes and milk, please?"

"Of course, sweetie."

Addy turned to go back inside and nearly bumped into Liberty, standing behind her. Liberty grasped Addy's arms to prevent the collision and smiled. The heat from Liberty's hands turned Addy's knees to rubber, and she stood still for a long moment, letting the sensation wash over her.

"Let me get it," Liberty offered, heading back into the house before Addy could reply.

"Who's that?" Tommy whispered.

"She's renting a room from us, Tommy. I think you'll like her, she's very nice."

"She looks like a flamingo."

"Tommy."

Liberty returned with the bowl of potatoes and a pitcher of milk. "What do I do?"

"Thanks, but I'll take care of it." Addy reached for the food.

"No, I'd really like to help."

"Caw! Caw!"

Tommy was running from one side of his house to the other, which he did when he was upset. She knew what was wrong.

"Tommy prefers that I feed him, because I'm his sister."

Addy put the food in the bucket, then hoisted it up by a pulley system rigged to an upper branch. This guy was a real fruitcake, Liberty said to herself, and so close to the murder scene. Earlier that day she had met with the deputy, who had briefed her on the location of the body on the Cooper property. It was too coincidental that a crazy guy lived within yards of where the reporter was found. She didn't know if the murder was connected to the radioactive-spill angle. That would take time. But a grown man who lived in a tree and made bird calls deserved closer scrutiny.

"Well, we should go back inside," Addy reminded her.

"But it's such a beautiful evening. I hate being cooped up. Won't you join me?" Liberty sat in the tree swing and patted the seat next to her.

Tiny alarm bells rang in Addy's body at the idea of being next to Liberty. As if in acknowledgment, a small fireworks explosion in the sky burst into a rosette of green and red. The already-warm evening became even warmer, and a flush rose from her neck to her cheeks. It would be rude to say no, and a very large part of her wanted to say yes. She cautiously approached and sat next to her boarder.

"There, now, that's nice, isn't it?" Liberty asked, smiling down at Addy.

Addy nodded, her throat suddenly dry. Liberty's thigh just barely touched hers, and she swore Liberty inched closer. Was Liberty coming on to her? Her heart was pounding and she suddenly felt shy. It had been a long time since someone had flirted with her, and she allowed herself the pleasure.

Liberty stretched her arm along the back of the swing. This was almost too easy. But unlike with Dee-Dee, she couldn't rush things with Addy. She couldn't afford to risk being shut out from what was happening with Addy's brother. If he was responsible for the recent activity in Deale, she'd need the help of his sister, which would be tricky indeed. Naturally she would want to protect him. But Liberty needed to find the source of the radioactive material.

"Your brother is okay up there?"

"He's fine." Addy squirmed. "He has everything he needs— heat in winter, electricity, water, food—everything that we enjoy down here. Except for a television and a phone. He had a TV early on but didn't watch it or want it, and the phone, well, obviously he didn't need that either. He does have an intercom up there and can call me any time."

"Could I go up and see him sometime?"

Addy hesitated. "Why?"

"For one thing, I've had my share of living in a tree." Liberty laughed at the memory of seeing angry frustration in the loggers' eyes. "Tommy and I have that in common. It would be fun to discuss the pros and cons, although he certainly has a lot more amenities than I had at the time."

"I don't know. Tommy is selective about who he allows up there. He used to let only Grandma and me, and I think Tommy's friend Jeff and Officer Kaczarowski have been up a few times."

"I see," Liberty said, noting the name Jeff and surprised to learn of the cop's personal interest in the Coopers. "And he never comes down?"

Addy abruptly rose. "I should get back to Fern and Chauncey. I'm sure they'll be gossiping about us by now. And I need to start clearing the table."

As Liberty strode back to the house, she dwelt on how uncomfortable Addy had been when she'd questioned her about her brother. She gazed up at the tree house, wondering if the guy was spying on her.

"I'm coming for you sooner or later, buddy."

❖

Karen drove out to the Cooper house early the next morning, intent on walking the crime scene again to see if she had missed anything. The ground had dried sufficiently, and she wanted to arrive when the tide was out in case something had been uncovered. Detectives had already canvassed the area, but it was her day off, and besides, she wanted to visit Addy.

She hadn't slept well, knowing the FBI agent had moved into Addy's house. She could spot a cad a mile away, and Liberty definitely fit the category. And after Dee-Dee had boasted of the great sex they'd had, Karen was doubly uncomfortable. Part of her wanted to warn Addy about the woman. She couldn't divulge Liberty's true identity, but it wasn't right that Addy was renting a room in her own home to someone who was being untruthful. And Addy didn't need to know that she was worried Liberty's charms would suck her in. The agent was an arrogant, narcissistic Casanova who needed taking down a notch.

Bypassing the house, Karen walked through the woods toward the shoreline. She turned away from the crime scene, scouring the beach for about a quarter mile. Returning the way she had come, she again passed the spot where the victim had been found and trekked a quarter mile down the other way.

Each time she studied the tall grass and, in some places, stamped them down to examine items she gleaned from the soil. They turned out to be seashells, rocks, rotting wood, or pieces of weathered glass. Frustrated at not finding anything, she finally ended her search back at the crime scene, digging through some of the mounds of dirt and weeds upturned in previous searches.

As the morning wore on and she began to sweat, she wished she'd brought some water. She sat on a piece of driftwood and removed her cap, wiping her forehead with her sleeve. Something thin and black was sticking out of the sand under a corner of the driftwood, and she plucked it from the sand and pulled. It came up easily, breaking the surface of the mud and trailing back under the wood. It was a strap, so she rose and pushed the log aside. She yanked hard, and out popped what appeared to be a camera case.

❖

Liberty had been keeping track of the deputy with binoculars ever since she began to walk along the beach. She couldn't make out what the officer had found, but she was itching to know. She had walked along the same beach, searching for clues, with no luck. How could the local hick deputy have located something she hadn't? She tossed the binoculars on the bed and went downstairs, where Addy was in the kitchen making breakfast.

"Good morning," Addy called cheerfully.

"Good morning." Liberty almost dashed out the back door but remembered her real purpose for renting the room and forced herself to slow down.

"Mmm, something smells good." She pressed into Addy's back as she stood frying bacon. "And I'm not talking about the French toast."

Addy's giggle made her smile. The pull in her stomach and the ache elsewhere signaled her need to get laid. Another couple of moments like these and she'd have Addy spread out before her like Christmas dinner. Seduce her, gain her trust, and then get to the bottom of things—in that order. She wanted her as soon as possible—partly because of the annoying deputy outside, and partly because she knew Addy would be a good lay.

"I'm going for a little walk before breakfast, if that's okay."

"Oh. Breakfast is almost ready, but I can hold it for a while. Chauncey is outside by the shrubs, making squirrels and rabbits out of them, and Fern is in the shower, so you have a little time."

Liberty could hear the wistfulness in her voice and knew Addy wanted her too. She almost reached around her, aching to fondle her breasts. But that move might frighten this little chicken. This situation called for a kiss, but now wasn't the right time.

"I'll be back before you can say lickety-split."

She was almost to the water's edge when she met Karen.

"Let's keep to the woods so we're not seen together," Liberty advised. "What did you find?"

"A camera case." Kazro, or whatever her name was, wiped off the front of it and showed her. "According to Vinson's editor, he had a Nikon F6."

"But where's the camera?"

"Yeah. Find the camera, and we just might come up with some interesting photos."

"That thing could be anywhere by now, Deputy. It could be in the bottom of the inlet, or the tide could've taken it out into the bay and the ocean beyond. Damn."

"Maybe. But it's worth having a couple of divers see what they can locate. We might get lucky."

Liberty eyed her skeptically. It was a pipe dream, but if the local police wanted to waste their time finding a needle in a haystack, that was fine with her. Addy's brother most likely had something to do with the crime, and she was going to pursue that lead. If Addy knew anything about her brother's involvement, she'd eventually extract it from her.

Liberty was known for getting her man, and in this case, she'd get the girl too. Only this time, it would be far more pleasurable.

Chapter Thirteen

Yo, Tommy," Jeff Olson yelled from the base of the red oak. "Can I come up?"

Tommy clambered onto the decking outside his front door. "Hi, Jeff. Sure."

While Jeff climbed the ladder, Tommy stared at the main house where Jeff's older brother and another guy were finishing painting the back. The scaffolding made the house look like it had a skeleton, only on the outside. Tommy wanted them to paint it purple, his favorite color, but Addy told him that Grandma had always liked yellow. And since it was already that color, that made sense to Tommy, so he agreed.

"I brought you some comics." Jeff wheezed as he sat on the deck. After pulling an inhaler from his front pocket, he sucked the medication like he was blowing up a balloon.

"Wow, Spider-Man." Tommy sat next to Jeff and flipped through the pages. "Thanks, Jeff."

Jeff handed Tommy a bubblegum ball, and for a while they competed to see who could blow the biggest bubble.

"Hey, I've got something to show you, but you gotta come inside." Tommy motioned Jeff to follow him.

Seated at the table, Tommy pulled the camera out from under the bed.

"Cool. Where'd you get it?"

"I found it."

"You found it? Whattya mean, you found it? It was just laying around up here in the tree branches? Come on, Tommy. It's your sister's, ain't it?"

"Nope. I told you, I found it."

"Yeah, right. You know if you found it, you're supposed to give it back to whoever lost it, right? Because it ain't yours."

Tommy thought hard about that. He couldn't give it back, so what was he supposed to do? Addy said he couldn't tell anybody about the man either, so he couldn't explain to Jeff how he got it.

"So is there any film in it?" Jeff asked.

Tommy shrugged. "I don't know how to work it."

"Here, let me show you." Jeff took the camera. "I got one last year for my birthday, but it's an automatic and a lot smaller than this." After a few minutes of pressing buttons and turning the lens, he said, "There's supposed to be a button to open this so I can see if it's got film, but I can't find it. I can ask Dale."

"No. You can't talk to your brother about it." Tommy was worried that a grown-up like Dale would make him explain where he got it, and Addy would be mad at him.

"Why not?"

"Because it's a secret." Tommy folded his arms across his chest and refused to say any more.

"Aw, come on," Jeff begged. "You can tell me. I'm your best friend, ain't I?"

Tommy hadn't thought about that. Jeff *was* his best friend, and they always shared everything. Tommy almost gave in. Addy said he shouldn't tell anybody, but Jeff wouldn't say anything.

"Tommy. Breakfast." Addy's voice came over the intercom.

Tommy stared at Jeff, his heart pounding like a drum. "It's Addy. She'd be mad if she found out I let you in on the secret."

"So your sister gets to know, but not your best friend." Jeff stood up. "If that's how you're gonna be, I'm going to help my brother. I get an allowance when I help, and then I can buy more comic books. See if I give you any."

Tommy followed him out to the deck as he climbed down. He didn't want Jeff to leave and was upset that he was mad at him. And now he wouldn't get any new comics. Maybe if he made Jeff swear that he wouldn't tell a soul, then he might tell him.

"Hi, Jeff," Addy said as he passed by.

"Hi."

The sullen greeting surprised Addy, and she noticed Tommy's forlorn expression, so they must have had an argument.

"Everything okay up there?"

"Jeff's mad at me." Tommy slowly pulled the rope for his breakfast, the pulley squealing in protest.

"How come?"

"'Cause I won't tell him the secret."

Addy caught her breath. Rushing to the tree, she scrambled to the top. "Tommy, you promised you wouldn't say anything to anyone, including Jeff. Remember?"

"But, Addy, Jeff is my best friend. And he won't bring me any more comic books if I don't."

"I'll bring you lots of comic books, Tommy, but you can't let Jeff know anything about the man you found. You can't tell anyone, ever, unless I say it's okay. Please, Tommy. This is very important. You have to promise me."

"Oh, all right," Tommy said, taking a bite of his pancake. "I promise. But I don't want Jeff to be mad at me no more."

"Don't worry. I'll talk to Jeff."

As she hugged Tommy, she noticed movement along the tree line near the house. Liberty and Karen were talking in the shadows.

"Tommy, where are your binoculars?"

"In there." Tommy gestured inside and continued to eat.

Addy found them lying on the table and focused on the spot

she had last seen the two women. Karen held something in her hand that she couldn't quite make out. What in the world could they be saying? Eventually they broke off, and Liberty headed toward the house while Karen continued along the trees. Back on the ground, Addy met Liberty in the yard.

"Am I too late for breakfast?" she asked.

"No. Fern and Chauncey are already eating. What were you and Karen talking about? I didn't realize you knew each other."

"Who?" Liberty paled.

"Officer Kaczarowski. I saw you two talking in the woods. What's she doing out here this early?"

"Oh, her, uh, well, we don't know each other. I just met her on my walk. She said she was investigating some murder that happened down by the inlet. Addy, you didn't tell me anything about a murder."

A knot formed in Addy's stomach. "Well, no. That's because it doesn't have anything to do with us. It just happened to occur on our land, that's all. And I don't want to get mixed up in it."

"I see. And how do you know Officer Kaza, Kazro, Karen?"

Addy wasn't sure she wanted to admit to knowing Karen at all, let alone *how* she knew her.

"Oh, come on, now, Addy. You're blushing. Is there more to you and the good deputy than meets the eye?"

"Absolutely not." Addy was flustered that the truth was obviously so evident on her face. "It was a long time ago, and besides, it's over."

At that moment, Karen appeared from out of the trees carrying a plastic garbage bag.

"Good morning, Addy." Karen could see the remnants of a blush on Addy's face, and her temper flared. Angry, she glared at Liberty.

"Good morning, Officer." Liberty stepped forward. "We were just talking about you, and I told Addy I bumped into you on my walk."

Karen was tempted to put the agent on the hot seat. She didn't like the way Liberty stood so close to Addy they almost touched. The intimate contact had to flagrantly violate an ethical code somewhere.

"Addy saw us talking in the woods," Liberty hastily added. "I'm new to town and surprised that such a thing could happen in such a small community. Is this type of crime common in Deale, Deputy? Is it safe to be here?"

Karen narrowed her gaze. Liberty was getting on her last nerve, and the smug expression she now wore irritated the hell out of her.

"Quite safe, I assure you. We haven't had a capital crime in this area in ages. Of course, if you're afraid—"

"Hardly," Liberty stated flatly.

Addy had the odd feeling that she had stepped into the middle of something between the two physically similar women— athletic, with dark hair and healthy suntans. And both were deadly attractive, a combination Addy found difficult to resist.

"I'd be happy to escort you home at night," Karen continued. "It's no trouble at all. I'm used to helping defenseless women."

Addy felt Liberty bristle beside her. She didn't know Liberty that well, but she knew Karen well enough to recognize her taunting. For some reason, these two didn't like each other, and she realized that it might be because of her. Having two women fight over her was so romantic.

"Well," Addy cheerfully said, "we were just about to sit down to breakfast, Officer. Would you care to join us?"

"I'd love to." Karen gave Liberty a smug smile. "Let me put this in the car."

Addy gazed at the bag. "Did you find something?"

"I'm not sure, but I'm taking it in anyway. Be right back."

Liberty took Addy's arm and, once inside, pulled out her chair, sat beside her, and leaned in suggestively.

"I'm starving," she said to Addy, a glimmer in her eyes.

Nervous, Addy smiled, glancing at Fern and Chauncey, who

were busily eating and reading the morning paper. Fern looked up when Karen sat down.

"Deputy," she said, "according to the morning paper, there are no suspects in the murder. Is that true, or are you keeping mum on the subject?"

"Unfortunately, Miss Bush, it's true. We're still investigating, though, and I'm sure we'll find whoever did it soon."

"Well, I hope we can keep the publicity to a minimum." Fern sniffed. "Lord knows what it would do to tourism if it got out. We sure don't want to make a federal case out of it."

Karen gazed at Liberty. "In fact, the feds are already involved." Liberty's head nearly snapped off when she jerked her neck. "A couple of agents visited yesterday. They're interested in what Scott Vinson was investigating when he died."

Addy almost spilled the coffee she was pouring into Liberty's cup. The FBI was in Deale. Her hands began to shake and her heart skipped erratically. They weren't local people. They would want to know about everyone in the area and where they were that night. Karen had deflected the scrutiny away from Tommy, but now they would come with all their advanced equipment and questions. She *had* to keep them away from Tommy.

"Hey, let me take that." Liberty held Addy's arm, placing the pot on the table. "You're trembling. Are you cold, or is it me?"

Liberty's wolfish leer made Addy tingle. Her skin burned where Liberty touched her and her blood ran hot through her body. She wasn't sure whether she was trembling because she was afraid or because Liberty was so near.

"There *is* a chill in the air this morning," Karen observed, looking like she would like to reach across the table and remove Liberty's hand from Addy's arm permanently. "How long did you say you were going to be in town, Liberty?"

"Oh, for a while." She gazed up at Addy. "I'm beginning to like the scenery, a lot."

"Well, there's a lot to see in Deale, Miss McDonald," Fern

said. "I lead a small group of birdwatchers along the shore and into the woods. Perhaps you'd care to join us?"

"I love birds," Liberty said, her attention still fixed on Addy. "They're so soft, and delicate, and I especially love to hear them sing."

Fern chuckled. "I knew I liked you."

"There's a pet store in town," Karen snidely suggested. "Why don't you go buy one? I hear the shops down by the docks have especially colorful ones."

"Down by the docks?" Fern asked. "There aren't any pet stores there, Deputy. And certainly no birds of particular interest, except for some common seagulls. Besides, the docks are a disgraceful part of town, Miss McDonald. Women of questionable character loiter there, if you know what I mean."

"*Sí.*" Chauncey spoke up for the first time.

"I prefer my birds wild and free." Liberty stared at Karen. "I've never had to pay for them."

"My cousin owns a pet shop," Fern added. "I'm sure she could get you any bird you like at a reasonable price."

"I don't believe your cousin has pigeons for sale, Miss Bush," Karen added.

"Okay," Addy said. She was feeling uncomfortable with Karen and Liberty's conversation and began to clear the table. Only Fern and Chauncey remained oblivious to the tension in the room, and Addy realized she should defuse the situation before it erupted.

"I'd best be getting to work anyway." Karen rose from her chair. "Addy, can I talk to you a minute?"

Addy glanced at Liberty, who made no move to leave the room.

"In the kitchen?" Karen suggested.

Once there, Addy placed a stack of dirty dishes by the sink and waited for Karen to speak.

"You better be careful about that one in there." Karen pointed her chin to the dining room and Liberty. "She's not someone you should be fooling around with."

Addy's anger bubbled up at the suggestion that she was fooling around with Liberty—not that she hadn't considered it. But Karen telling her what to do especially galled her.

"It's really none of your business, *Officer*, whom I choose to fool around with. What right do you have to tell me that, after what you did?"

"Oh, geez, not that again." Karen sagged against the counter. "Forget I said anything. Addy, I'd really like to move on. I was hoping you'd agree to have dinner with me soon. Nothing more than that. Just a chance to sit down over a meal and talk. I'd like to be friends again. Please?"

Karen's plaintive expression moved Addy, and for a brief, aching moment she wanted to alleviate Karen's discomfort. It wouldn't hurt to have dinner with her, one time. The attraction was still there, and she wished she could recapture what they'd had before. She wanted to trust again. Still, she hesitated, unwilling to give in too easily.

"Well, why don't you give me a call next week?"

Karen smiled. "I will. Thanks, Addy."

The kitchen suddenly felt too small, and Addy resisted her body's overwhelming desire to press into Karen's. After saying a quick good-bye, Karen closed the kitchen door behind her, waved hello to Tommy, then disappeared around the corner of the house.

Addy wanted to run after her, call her back and tell her she also wanted to be friends, to be more than friends. But her feet wouldn't move, and neither would her mind. She was stuck in time, and she needed to find a way to the future.

Chapter Fourteen

Clarence burst through the back door, his expression as wild as the Atlantic during a hurricane.

"The feds are in town, the feds are in town," he shouted as he stormed to the kitchen and tossed the groceries onto the counter. "What're we gonna do, Frank?"

"Are you sure?" Abel stepped timidly from the living room, a cigarette dangling from his lips. "How do you know?"

"It's all over town, everybody's talking about it." Clarence slammed the door and locked it. "They're probably investigating the murder, Frank. They're gonna figure out sooner or later what happened."

"Shut up and quit running around like a moron." Frank tossed his beer can into the trash and sat at the table. "Nobody's gonna figure out nothin' if you keep your mouth shut and stop acting guilty."

"I'm not taking the rap alone," Clarence roared, the tendons red and prominent on his thick neck. "We're all in this together. If I go down, we all go down."

The room went silent. The only sound was the blinds tapping at the window as they blew gently in the wind. Frank rose from his chair and limped to within inches of Clarence's face.

"You don't want to threaten me, Clarence," he said calmly. "That would not be the smart thing to do."

They stood glaring at each other, until Clarence blinked.

"That reporter was small fish compared to what I have in mind." Frank took another beer out of the refrigerator. "Our main goal is to inflict as much damage on Washington as we can. I want to scare the shit out of them, and if a few bureaucrats get taken out in the process, so much the better. If I can put together a big enough explosive to get their attention, then maybe some justice will get done."

"You can get your revenge if you want to," Clarence muttered, "but I don't want to go to prison for this."

"I told you. Nothin's gonna happen if you keep your mouth shut. They have no reason to suspect us unless you go and do something stupid. But just in case, I'm gonna put this equipment away for a while until things quiet down. I'm not in any hurry."

Frank gazed out the window to the inlet beyond. He wondered why the feds would be in Deale, if what Clarence said was true. They wouldn't be out here just to investigate a murder. Something else had tipped them off, but how did they know he was up to something? They might not realize it was him specifically, but they were aware something was going on. How? He reviewed everything he'd done up to this point but could think of nothing to draw attention. They'd burned the parts he hadn't been able to use. No traces of anything were left.

It was just as well that he stopped working on his project for a while. The feds would be snooping around the inlet and probably come calling. Maybe he ought to send Clarence away for a few days, to cool him off and keep him away from any questions that might come their way. If that idiot spoiled things before he got his chance to set off his bomb, he'd kill him. Clarence was getting on his nerves anyway.

❖

"No, no, no," Fern admonished, rising from her lounge chair. "A platypus has the bill of a duck, Mr. Velasquez. Yours resembles a French horn."

She strode to the crape myrtle and pointed to the snout Chauncey was trimming.

"You need to thin this out and lengthen it, make it flatter. You see?" She grasped the area in question and smashed it together with her hands.

"Ah, Señora Bush. You break the tree." He grasped her hands and gently pried them from the myrtle. "It is not a platypus, it is a squirrel."

"A squirrel? Well, no wonder I couldn't recognize it. Why didn't you say so in the first place?"

Liberty noticed the two arguing in the backyard, but kept her gaze on the red oak and the tree house above. She eased toward the tree and began to climb. With Addy in town and the rest of the tenants otherwise occupied, she hurried to her destination. Scampering to the door, she quietly knocked.

"Tommy? It's me, Liberty. I moved into your house—I mean your sister's house. I was hoping you and I could talk."

She could detect no sound from within, but she knew he was in there. Everyone said he never left the tree, and the few nights she had checked from her bedroom window he hadn't. She admired the small house that seemed to blend in with the natural contours of the tree. Peeking through the branches, she could see the inlet and bay beyond, a spectacular view, and a clear sight line had been trimmed near the window. Had Tommy been able to see the reporter from up here? Had he gone down to the shore, threatened by a stranger in his territory? Had they fought and Tommy attacked?

She needed to get inside and meet the man, talk to him and learn what he was, or wasn't, capable of doing. Then she needed to find the connection between the radioactive waste in the Chesapeake and Tommy. Were the two incidents related? It was too coincidental not to think so.

"Tommy? It's okay. I just want to talk with you. Addy said it would be all right."

A sound on the other side of the door gave her hope.

"I lived in a tree once too. I didn't have a nice house like this, but the tree was big and beautiful, and I wanted to save it from some bad men who wanted to chop it down. That's what I do, Tommy. I keep trees and other things from being hurt. I want to help you too, Tommy. I don't want anything bad to happen to you. Like what happened to the man down by the water."

She waited a while longer, and just as she was about to give up, the lock in the door turned. A young man in his early twenties, with light brown hair and hazel eyes, stood inside the door. He was thin and pale, not delicately so, but in a way that fit the frame he was born with.

"Addy said it was okay?"

"Sure, like I said. Can I come in?"

Tommy hesitated, appearing timid, afraid, and uncertain. His mental age was probably at most half his real age. If he was indeed childlike, she would need to treat him as such.

"How about I tell you about the time I was living in the big old redwood tree in California and it started to rain?" As Liberty eased into the house, Tommy backed up cautiously and stood by his bedside. "Mind if I sit down at your table here?"

Tommy shook his head, and as she sat, she noticed the clear view of the inlet and a small house in the distance, a tractor stuck in the mud near its banks. He could see everything.

"You have a very nice place. I can understand why you wouldn't want to ever come down."

Tommy averted his eyes and she wondered at his evasiveness. Was he simply afraid of her? She could use that to her advantage.

"You don't ever leave the tree, right, Tommy?"

"You said you were going to talk about the tree you lived in."

"I will. I'll tell you all about it, but I just want to ask you a few questions first. Then you can ask me all the questions you want about my tree. Okay?"

When he didn't say anything, she continued. "I lived in a

redwood tree in California. A redwood tree is really tall, a lot taller than your tree, Tommy. But my tree was in a big forest and I couldn't see much where I was. You can see a long way out your window at the water and the shore."

"Mr. Velasquez cut the branches so I could."

Liberty tucked that bit of information away. So Chauncey Velasquez had been up here too? Addy said only a couple of people had ever been in the tree house. She hadn't mentioned Chauncey. Did Tommy want a better view, or was it Chauncey? Or was it Addy?

"That was nice of him. I'm sure that made it so much better. Did you see anything the day Scott Vinson, the reporter, was killed?"

"Caw! Caw!" Tommy shouted, and jumped onto his bed, bouncing from one end to the other and flapping his arms.

This guy was a total freak. Shit. She didn't have her service revolver. If he went berserk and attacked her, she'd have a tough time fending him off in this confined space. Liberty got up and inched toward the door, never turning her back on him. Hearing a noise outside, she glimpsed Addy's car moving down the road. She didn't want Addy to be pissed off at her for coming up here, and she needed to calm Tommy down quickly.

"Sorry, buddy, sorry. I didn't mean to upset you. I'm leaving now, okay? I just want to be friends. I want to talk, that's all."

Tommy stopped flapping his arms and stood still in the middle of his bed.

"That's right, see? Everything's going to be just fine. We'll talk another time, I promise."

Liberty grabbed the doorknob and yanked it. Hurrying to the ladder, she nearly slid the entire way down.

"Now that resembles a swan," Fern pronounced.

"It is a seahorse," Chauncey argued, taking a bite out of the tree with his large pruning shears.

Liberty casually strolled through the yard and observed Chauncey with the potential weapon in his hands. He snipped and sliced with confidence, the cords in his forearms standing out from years of hard work on fishing boats. His dossier stated that he seemed to have no family and had moved to the Cooper house shortly before the murder. She needed to corner him soon.

CHAPTER FIFTEEN

Though Karen couldn't hear what the two FBI agents talking with the chief were saying, she could see the expressions on their faces through the glass windows of the sheriff's office. Just what this town needed, more feds. The diner gossip said they were here investigating the Vinson murder, but Karen knew the real reason. Still, it bothered her that the townspeople believed the department needed help to solve the crime. Almost a week had passed and the trail was getting cold.

She got up and poured herself another cup of coffee, still keeping an eye on the men in the office. She had been the one to find the camera case, their first real break, and it had definitely belonged to Vinson. The department was assembling a team to dredge the waters near the Cooper shoreline to try to find the camera, and hopefully they would. But would the film be viable and show anything worthwhile?

Her phone rang and she answered immediately.

"It's Liberty. Can you talk?"

"Go ahead." Karen sat at her desk.

"I just met the Cooper boy. I was—"

"You what?" Karen shot out of her chair.

"I went to see him. Man, what a wacko. He was flying around the room like a seven forty-seven when I left him. He was pretty calm at first, but when I mentioned Vinson, he went off. I'm telling you, the kid knows something."

"Shit, McDonald. What the hell did you do that for? Tommy doesn't leave the tree house and he freaks out when strangers are around. You can't go messing with him like that."

"I'll do whatever it takes to get to the bottom of this thing. If he had something to do with the murder, then we'll get a warrant and check out the Cooper place to see what else we can find."

"Tommy? There's no way in hell he had anything to do with it."

"If he didn't, there's nothing for you to worry about, is there, Deputy? It'll take a lot of work to get it out of him, but we will. The FBI has all kinds of shrinks on staff."

Karen collapsed into her chair and pressed a fist to her throbbing head. She needed to regain control of this investigation. She'd drive out to the Coopers' right away and talk to Tommy before it was too late.

❖

"Here, let me help you with that," Liberty offered. She took two bags from Addy, carried them into the house, and set them on the kitchen table.

"Thanks." Addy groaned. "I had a lot to get at the hardware store today. I want Dale to replace some broken hinges and doorknobs, and fix some other things around here when he's done painting the house. He's doing a great job, don't you think?"

"Yes. It must be tiring to be responsible for this big place and a brother who, well, who needs a lot of attention."

"Tell me about it. I get sore just from climbing up and down the tree."

"Turn around," Liberty ordered. When Addy hesitatingly obliged, Liberty placed her hands on Addy's shoulders and began to massage them.

"Oh, God, that feels good." Addy sighed and dropped her head.

"That's right, let it go." Liberty ran her hands up and down Addy's back and shoulders. She traced a line from Addy's neck to her waist, then let her hands slip to the front of Addy's stomach and gently pulled Addy into her. She kissed her neck and shoulders while she rubbed gentle circles. When Addy relaxed against her and her head fell back, Liberty nibbled the underside of her jaw. She let her hands roam farther north and cupped Addy's breasts, stroking them with her thumbs.

"Oh, yes," Addy hissed.

Liberty smiled. It wouldn't be long now. The tug in her belly made her even more eager to get Addy between the sheets. It was there she discovered the most important secrets about a woman. And she would discover Addy's. Once Addy opened up to her, so to speak, Liberty would be able to get her to talk about Tommy. She wanted to know more about his mental capacity and any violent tendencies. She'd have the two new agents in town dig into any police records concerning him.

Movement outside the window caught Liberty's eye, and she was surprised to see Karen striding rapidly toward the house. This was going to be good. The back door was open, with only the screen door separating them from the outside. Would Karen stop to knock? At the moment, she resembled a charging bull, blind to all but the red cape in front of her. True to Liberty's prediction, Karen barged into the kitchen without stopping.

Addy leapt from Liberty's arms, hastily pulled her knit top down, and tucked a loose strand of hair behind her ear.

"Karen. Hi, we were just, uh…"

Karen was so angry, and so intent on talking to Addy, even though she didn't know what she would say, that she was stunned to find her in Liberty's arms. She almost threw a punch at Liberty. She clenched and unclenched her fist, and her body shook so violently she had to stop and force herself to calm down.

"What are you doing, Addy?" Karen asked through clenched teeth.

"Afternoon, Officer. Is there a problem?" Liberty asked.

Her smug expression infuriated Karen because she couldn't say or do anything about it. She couldn't warn Addy any more than she already had about Liberty, and she certainly couldn't tell her that Liberty was with the FBI, possibly investigating her and her brother. If Addy learned who she really was, she'd kick her out of her house and blow her cover, and Karen would probably lose her job. Liberty knew exactly what she was doing by seducing Addy, but she was going too far.

"No *problem*, Ms. McDonald. Addy, we need to talk. Come on." Karen held the screen door open for her.

"Excuse me, *Officer*?" Addy bristled. "Are you ordering me into the backyard?"

Karen momentarily controlled her anger, though it took every ounce of her strength.

"I'm sorry. Would you please come outside? I have something important to discuss with you."

"Excuse me, Liberty," Addy said.

"Certainly." Liberty smiled warmly at her.

Addy stalked out into the yard but didn't stop. She was angry at Karen for insinuating that she had staked a claim on her—and at herself for having been caught in such a compromising position. Liberty's caresses aroused yet embarrassed her. It would serve Karen right after what happened with Miss Wilson, but why did she feel so guilty when Karen saw her with Liberty?

Karen caught up with her, grabbed her shoulder, and spun her around, snapping, "What the hell do you think you're doing with her?"

"What the hell business is it of yours?" Addy snapped back. She wished Karen would remove her hand from her shoulder. The heat that seeped into her skin and Karen's nearness set her body on fire. Some of their best lovemaking had been make-up sex. Just the memory of some of those encounters made her weak.

"I thought we were going out next week."

"What of it? We're having a friendly dinner, nothing more."

"Addy, you know I want more than that."

"Well, your chances are going from slim to none if you keep this up. You have no right to tell me who I can see."

"Okay, all right." Karen held up her hands defensively. She took a deep breath and released it slowly. "That's not why I came. I want to talk to Tommy."

Addy's anger deflated and she was instantly wary. "Tommy? What for?"

"I need to ask him a few questions. Don't worry. It's nothing. Tommy trusts me. I've spent most of my life around him. If he gets upset, I'll stop."

"What are you going to ask him about?" Addy glanced up at the tree house. "I told you, he doesn't know anything."

"We need to be certain. Better me than someone else. And I assure you, if the feds find out about Tommy, they won't ask permission. Please, Addy."

"I'll go with you."

"No. I need to do this alone. Otherwise, Tommy might think he's being punished in some way and refuse to answer. You know I care about Tommy. I won't let anything happen to him. Let me help him, Addy."

Worry crept back into Addy's gut. She had believed it had left for good, but she had only been deluding herself. Karen was right. If not her, someone else would come along sooner or later. She couldn't speak, but nodded her assent. Karen was the only person she would trust with Tommy's feelings.

Karen was knocking on Tommy's door before Addy could change her mind.

"Tommy, it's me, Karen," she called, and he let her in quickly and closed the door.

"I know Liberty was up here. And I know she scared you, but I promise I won't let her near you again."

"I don't like her," Tommy said, barely above a whisper.

"That makes two of us. What did she ask you about?"

Tommy hesitated. "The man."

"The man who died down by the inlet, right? What did you say?"

Tommy walked to his bed and sat down. "I'm hungry."

"I'll get you something in a minute." His avoidance exasperated her. "Tommy, did you see the man get hurt? Do you know anything that can help me? Please, Tommy, you need to tell me, okay? I thought we were friends, and that we could say anything to each other. No secrets, right?"

"But Addy told me to keep it a secret, from everybody."

Karen turned cold and everything went still, like the winds calming before a tornado. She had difficulty getting air into her lungs and walked to the window to breathe deeply.

"Why does she want you to keep it a secret? I don't understand." Karen's voice sounded far away, even to herself.

"I was going to tell Jeff about it, but Addy got mad. She said not to say anything to him and not to tell you either. Then she brought me some comic books. I got the Fantastic Four and Batman…"

Tommy kept talking, but Karen wasn't listening, unable to comprehend what was happening. She tried to clear her mind of all the noises inside it. Something wasn't right. She couldn't believe what she was hearing. Tommy must be confused, that's all. It was all make-believe and he didn't understand what he was saying.

But she recalled when the police were questioning Addy, how strangely she behaved during the entire investigation. Karen had wanted to believe she was simply upset because of the body on her property, but she could kick herself now for not letting someone question Tommy. She had lost valuable time in the investigation, but suddenly she felt in no hurry to solve the crime.

"Thanks, Tommy. I'll go get you something to eat now."

She trudged to the deck and slowly climbed to the ground, with each step the weight on her growing heavier.

"What did he say?" Addy asked.

"Nothing. Nothing of importance. I need to get back to work. I'll call you later."

Tommy watched Karen head to the police car parked in the driveway.

"Man, no wonder you didn't want me to know," Jeff said as he crawled out from underneath the bed.

"You can't tell anybody," Tommy begged tearfully. "Addy'll get mad at me. I promised her I wouldn't tell you or Karen, and now I broke my promise."

"Don't worry, I'm keeping my mouth shut. Now that Deputy Kaczarowski knows, we don't need to tell anybody else."

CHAPTER SIXTEEN

Karen had been nursing her glass of beer for an hour at the Happy Harbor, letting it grow warm and flat. Sometimes she thought about Addy, other times about nothing at all. For the first time she didn't know what to do, which unsettled her. In the army she simply followed orders but used her brain to make decisions regarding those orders. In civilian life, she still followed orders, but she had much more leeway to carry them out. She had to report her latest findings, but she didn't want to.

She had known Addy and Tommy so long they were her family, even if Addy didn't choose to view them that way. Karen could no more suspect them than she could her own mother. But what had Tommy meant by keeping Vinson a secret? She couldn't interrogate Tommy. She needed to talk to Addy, find out what he meant. But what about Addy's behavior that day and her appearance of guilt? Was Karen missing something?

"If you don't pick your chin up off my bar soon I'm going to lose every customer in the joint." Dee-Dee swiped a bar towel across the surface, placing a coaster under Karen's glass. "And keep the damn glass on a coaster, will ya? It's bad enough the men put cigarette burns on the counter."

Karen gazed at Dee-Dee as she sucked on her cigarette butt, letting the ashes drift to the floor. "Didn't you give those up for Euell Gibbons?"

Dee-Dee snorted. "She kindly mentioned the cigarette smell to me. Of course, that was after the sex. But damn, she was awesome in bed."

"Please, spare me the details."

"What bug crawled up your ass tonight?"

"Aw, nothing." Karen wished she could talk to someone.

"It's Addy, isn't it?"

"What makes you say that?" Karen squinted at her through the smoke.

"Damn, woman. You ain't been right since she got back in town. You've been in love with her since the first lungfish crawled onto land. What did she do? Give you the same old song about how you broke her heart? Well, you did, hon. Being cheated on is tough to get over."

"Jesus, Dee-Dee. We've been through that a million times. You know how bad I feel about it. I've been punished enough. For Christ's sake, it's been over six years. Why can't she move on?"

Dee-Dee shrugged. "Addy's stuck in the past. She hasn't had it easy since she was a kid, what with her folks gone and now her grandma. On top of all that, she's got to be responsible for Tommy."

God, Karen hadn't considered that. If Addy was somehow mixed up in this, what would happen to Tommy? *If* Addy was mixed up in this. No wonder she didn't want Tommy to talk to anyone.

Hopefully, Tommy was confused and neither he nor Addy had anything to do with Vinson's murder, but her gut told her otherwise. Yet she couldn't let them down.

❖

The sun had just broken the edge of the horizon the next morning when Liberty strolled through the woods on the path that led to the inlet. Halfway there, she turned left on a diagonal route that she had discovered on her first hike. Within moments, she spotted the two men who stood out like cockroaches on a white linoleum floor.

"Cheatham, Grassley," she acknowledged.

"Agent McDonald," the husky blond, Agent Cheatham, said. "What've you got?"

"Here." She handed him a small packet. "Water samples from the area. They need to be analyzed. And I may have a suspect. The brother, Tommy Cooper."

"Huh?" Grassley asked.

"Exactly." Liberty leaned closer. "A little more time and I'll crack that nut. He's got something to do with this, and I'm just the agent to find out. Boys, take it to the bank. I'll have this case solved in no time—Cooper's our man."

Cheatham peeked at Grassley and shrugged. "Uh, whatever, McDonald. We're dropping by the Cooper house later. We're interviewing all the residents, including the brother. After that, we cross the inlet to talk to the Gripps."

"It's your time to waste, but I think the Gripps are a dead end. The Cooper girl is protecting her brother. I can smell it. The guy whacked the reporter in a fit of psychotic rage and then flew the coop." Liberty guffawed at her own joke.

"Well, we still have to talk to everybody in the area. We'll drop by the Coopers' in a little bit."

"Suit yourselves." Liberty turned to go. "But the girl is mine. Once I cozy up to her, I'll clip her brother's wings."

❖

"I told the police already. I was working at the library that day," Fern haughtily informed the husky FBI agent. "You can ask anyone there. What audacity to even question my integrity. Why, anyone informed on the subject, such as I am, could tell you that most murders are committed by young white males, typically loners. Are you married, Agent Cheatham?"

"No, ma'am."

"Do you live alone?"

"Yes, ma'am."

"See? You could be the murderer and no one would ever suspect. In fact, it would be the perfect cover—you investigating a crime that you committed. Ooh, I read a mystery like that. Who wrote it? I think I have the book upstairs—"

"Miss Bush," Agent Cheatham said, "I believe we have everything we need. Thanks for your help. If we have any further questions, we'll be in touch."

"You do that, Agent. I once attended a dinner and interactive murder mystery in Elkridge and solved the crime right away. I can help if you like."

"Thank you again, Miss Bush, we'll let you know." Agent Cheatham rose from his chair and motioned his partner and Addy to the hallway.

Addy indicated the next door down from Fern's. "This is Mr. Velasquez's room."

Agent Cheatham tapped on the door. "Mr. Velasquez? FBI."

They waited several moments, but heard no sound from within.

"I told him you would be talking to him, but maybe he didn't understand. He could be out in the garden working."

"Do you have a key to the room?" Agent Cheatham asked.

"Yes." Addy hesitated. "But I don't like to go invade my tenants' privacy without their permission."

The door handle turned easily in Cheatham's hand. Without waiting for Addy's permission, he stuck his head into the room.

"Um, is this legal?" Addy asked.

Cheatham glared at her. "Let's see if he's outside, then."

They checked the front and back of the house, but Chauncey wasn't in sight.

"That's really odd," Addy said. "He was here a little while ago."

"We'll come back another time." Cheatham wrote in a notepad. "Now we'd like to speak to your brother, Ms. Cooper."

"Tommy?" Addy's heart thumped roughly. She had feared they would get to this point, but had hoped they might forget.

"Is that a problem?" Grassley stared at her.

"No. It's just that, well, my brother is handicapped. And he's easily excitable. I don't want him to get upset over things he knows nothing about. Can't you simply ask me the questions? Everybody knows Tommy doesn't come down out of his tree house, so there's no reason to question him." Addy inhaled deeply after speaking in one hurried breath.

"Don't worry, we'll be careful," Cheatham assured her. "We can take Tommy into the local hospital and have a psychiatrist present."

"No! Absolutely not." Addy was shaking and couldn't stop. She glanced furtively for an escape route.

"Then let us go up and talk to him, Ms. Cooper," Grassley said. "We'll be as quick as possible."

She reluctantly agreed, praying Tommy would remember his promise.

Crowded into the tree house, the two agents hunched over as though they had drunk the "Big" liquid from *Alice in Wonderland*. Tommy squeezed into the corner, and Addy sat next to him on the bed, resting her hand on his knee.

"Hello, Tommy," Cheatham said after they sat at the table.

"Tommy, these men are from the FBI—sort of like the police. They want to ask you a few questions and then they'll leave you alone. Okay?" Addy petted him, but his body remained tightly coiled.

"Tommy," Cheatham said, "you know about the reporter who was found down by the inlet last week. We want to find out what you know about it. Did you see anything or anyone that day?"

Tommy turned to Addy and she desperately wanted to help him. Instead she made soothing sounds and spoke softly, telling him everything would be all right.

"Tommy?" Cheatham repeated.

Tommy shook his head and mumbled, "I don't know."

He jumped up on his bed and flapped his arms up and down, but Addy climbed up beside him and pulled them to his sides.

"It's okay, Tommy. No one is going to hurt you. I'm here."

The two agents stared at each other, and Addy knew they were out of their depth.

"Like I said, ask anybody. Tommy doesn't leave this house. He doesn't have any information, and neither do I. Now, please. Can we go back?"

"We'll leave it for now, Ms. Cooper, but if we need anything else, we'll call."

The two agents left and Addy remained seated on the bed, drained from even that brief encounter. If they did return, she didn't think she could take it. And if she couldn't, how would Tommy?

❖

"Well?" Liberty asked. She sat on a tree stump in the woods, peeling off the loose bark and casually chewing it.

"You were right," Cheatham admitted. "The guy's nuts. It'll take a shrink to get anything out of him. But he may not be able to help us. We're going to the Gripps' as planned. They could have seen something from across the inlet. It's the only other house visible from the Cooper home."

"Maybe." Liberty pulled a wooden thread from between her teeth. "Natural floss. I'll try to get up there and talk to him one more time. And if I can't get anything out of him, then it's the sister's turn. My nose tells me she's the bird we're after."

CHAPTER SEVENTEEN

S hit, shit, they're coming, Frank." Abel dashed from the front of the house to the back several times, a cloud of smoke trailing behind him. "It's the feds, I just know it. I can spot an unmarked car a mile away."

"Let me get my shotgun," Clarence growled. "We'll blow them to kingdom come before they even set foot outta that Chrysler. We'll mount their heads on the wall next to that big old bass I caught last summer."

"Better yet, let's blow them to pieces with a chunk of that C-4, huh, Frank?" Abel asked. "There'd be nothing left to find."

"Would you two get your heads out of your asses before they get here? Let's see what they're up to first." Frank hobbled to the kitchen window and peered out at the black sedan stopping out front. They were so obvious. They wouldn't last a heartbeat in the Gulf.

"They're comin' for us, Frank," Clarence exclaimed. "I ain't going to prison again, and sure as hell not for murder. I didn't do nothin' wrong."

"You're the one who jumped on top of the guy," Abel said.

"I tripped," Clarence insisted. "But I'm not the one who shoved the stick through him."

"Shut up," Frank yelled. "They're here."

After the two FBI agents identified themselves, Frank invited them inside. As their eyes scanned the house and the husky one glanced out the back window to the inlet beyond, Frank stood at the kitchen counter, his .357 Magnum in the drawer by his hand.

"So, have you found out who killed that poor guy?" he asked.

"Not yet, but we have some leads. We know the police asked you some questions, but would you recount where you were and what you were doing the day of the murder?" Cheatham sat on the couch and Grassley on the chair next to him.

Frank, Abel, and Clarence took turns telling the agreed-upon story. They were all watching the Orioles play the Yankees and didn't see or hear anything. Frank wanted to knock the crap out of Clarence for offering information beyond what he had told him to say. Clarence was hopping around and seemed so nervous Frank was afraid he would pee his pants.

"Have any of you found anything unusual on or around your property?" Grassley asked.

Frank shifted uncomfortably. "Like what?"

"We think the reporter had a camera with him at the time, but we can't be sure," Cheatham said.

Frank's heart stopped, then restarted. "Why would it be on our property? Seems to me if it's anywhere, it's on the property of the folks across the way."

"You're probably right," Cheatham said. "But we need to check every possibility. I doubt it would have washed up on shore if it had fallen into the inlet. It was too heavy. But the police plan to have divers out in the morning searching the waters. We're hoping to get lucky."

"Yeah, well, good hunting."

When the agents finished their questioning, Frank stood at the kitchen window as they slowly drove away.

"A camera. A fucking camera," Clarence shouted. He ran to the door as the agents' car bounced along the rutted road. "Now what the fuck are we gonna do, Frank? Huh? Mr. Brains has got all the answers, so what are we gonna do? That fucking reporter took pictures of us—of you putting together a bomb or something. Jesus Christ, what are we gonna do?"

"I swear to God, Clarence, I'm gonna fucking kill you if you don't shut the fuck up. That's what *I'm* gonna do." Frank struggled to within inches of Clarence and stared angrily at him. "They said they didn't know for sure if that guy had a camera with him, but *we* have to be sure. He didn't have anything on him when we got to him, but it could have fallen somewhere. Since they've searched every inch across the way, it could be on our land. If we don't find it first, Clarence, you could wind up sharing a cell with some guy who fancies dumb asses."

❖

Addy sat on the couch idly flipping through fabric swatches as Dee-Dee plopped down sample books. She was trying to brighten the kitchen with color and paint, a task she had been anticipating until now.

After a moment of stability, her life had once again derailed. Even after losing her job, Maureen, and her grandmother, she had believed she could start fresh in Deale with her brother. But now this had to happen. Tommy had nothing to do with the death of the reporter, but no one but her would believe him. So far she had managed to safeguard him from false accusations, and she hoped her luck would hold in at least this one area.

Then there was her confusion over Liberty and Karen. Liberty led such an exciting life traveling and fighting for what she believed in. Karen was, well, Karen—her first love. She was sexy as hell, but Addy couldn't get past the betrayal. After all these years, why couldn't she get Karen out of her bloodstream?

"Addy?"

"Huh?"

"I said, what do you think of this plaid? Hello? Where've you been?"

"Oh, uh, yes, that's nice, Dee-Dee."

"You're thinking about Karen."

"How did you know?"

"It hasn't been that long since you were all dreamy-eyed over her. Hell, I'm surprised you're the one who got through high school and went on to college. You didn't seem to pay much attention in class, especially if Karen was there. I busted my ass and my parents were thrilled if I brought home Cs."

"You never busted your ass studying in high school."

"I did if you count Mr. Peterson, who nearly broke his hand spanking me."

"Mr. Peterson spanked you? My God, what did you do?"

"I was a very naughty girl, and Mr. Peterson liked his girls naughty." Dee-Dee giggled and winked.

Addy rolled her eyes. "Geez, Dee-Dee."

"Hey. I graduated, didn't I? But enough about me, although it *is* my favorite subject. What's up with you and Karen? Why can't you two get along?"

"You know why." Addy picked up another book of swatches.

"Come on. You can't be serious. That old story about Miss Wilson—who, by the way, was pretty damn hot. Still is."

"You've seen her?"

"Seen her? I've slept with her. She's still teaching gym, and, for a woman her age, she still has a great ass."

"You see?" Addy snapped. "You and Karen are both so casual in your sexual relationships. It doesn't matter who it is. Whatever happened to monogamy, loyalty, respect?"

"Now wait a minute, Addy." Dee-Dee put her swatch book on the coffee table. "Don't go confusing Karen's one mistake years ago with my extracurricular activities. She's suffered enough, don't you think?"

"Suffered? Suffered? She broke my heart. I was—no, *still am*—hurt. Do you call sleeping with Miss Wilson suffering?"

"Well, no, now that you mention it—"

"I can't possibly see how Karen has suffered the way I have." Addy knew the pitch of her voice was steadily rising, but she couldn't help it.

"She's in love with you, you idiot. Can't you see that?"

Addy stared at her, trying to comprehend what she'd said. Why, Karen probably never gave her a second thought now, except when she tried to act all macho around Liberty. She was handsome, smart, and kindhearted, and she treated Tommy as though he was her own brother. She was a great catch. Surely she had found someone by now. Or perhaps she still wasn't interested in settling down with one person.

"Did she tell you that?" Addy asked softly.

"She didn't have to. All she's done since you left is talk about you, about the great times you two used to have. It's obvious in her face, in the way she looks at you. And, honey," Dee-Dee rested her hand on Addy's arm, "I see it in your face too. Whenever she's around, your eyes never leave her. You still love her, don't you."

It was a statement, not a question, and Addy wanted to say no. But she couldn't. It had taken her a long time to sift through the anger and hurt to discover the love still buried within. But was it too late to rescue what was left? Could she forgive Karen, or was it time to move on?

"You can't go home again."

Fern bustled into the room, a bolt of fabric under one arm. "Sure you can. You just can't have the same expectations. What are we talking about?"

"*We* are talking about nothing in particular," Dee-Dee said.

"I remember after the death of my first husband, Wilfredo— God rest his soul—I moved back into Mama's house. Ay-ay-ay, what a time that was. Mama had been all set to turn my bedroom into a tattoo parlor. Daddy was a sailor, you see, and Mama had insisted she be the only one to inflict that kind of pain on him. No going off to some distant port like Hong Kong to get an obscene tattoo that wouldn't come off. Of course, nowadays, you can have them removed. As a matter of fact, I read an interesting book about that recently. They actually take a laser and—"

"Fern," Addy said.

"Yes, dear. My point was that Mama didn't convert my room into a tattoo parlor after all. A year later I married Mario—God rest his soul too—and after Mama died, the house burned down. So you see, it all worked out in the end."

Addy tried to understand what Fern was saying, but it hurt her head too much, so she finally gave up.

"As I was saying," Dee-Dee continued, "aren't you two supposed to be going out to dinner soon?"

"Saturday. She's taking me to Petey Green's."

"So much better, and a lot more romantic than the Happy Harbor. Though I happen to like the type of instant mashed potatoes they use at the HH. But can't you see? She's trying to make amends, get back in your good graces. If you just give her a chance, it could be as good as or even better than it was before. At least try."

Addy wasn't sure Dee-Dee was right, but at least she could hear what Karen had to say. If Karen still cared for her, as Dee-Dee said, maybe she'd reformed. She would give Karen an opportunity to prove herself over dinner. After that, well, she'd just have to see.

"This fabric you selected for the kitchen curtains is lovely, dear," Fern said. "I can have these sewn up in no time. Has anyone seen Chauncey lately? He was supposed to fix that broken curtain rod, but he's not around."

Liberty entered the living room and flopped down on the sofa next to Addy, her shoulder touching hers. "The last I saw him was the day the FBI paid their visit," Liberty said. "Or, I should say, just before the FBI arrived. I wonder where he went."

"It *was* rather odd," Addy said. "I told him they were coming and he said he'd stay near the house. But then he disappeared." The heat from Liberty's shoulder seared her skin, bare in her sleeveless shirt. A distant throb flared to life and she crossed her legs to mute it.

"Interesting," Liberty said.

"Hiya, babycakes," Dee-Dee cooed, rising from her chair to sit on the armrest. She stretched out across the back of the couch and tousled Liberty's hair. "Whatcha been up to?"

Liberty was torn between visually devouring the voluptuous cleavage thrust upon her and her desire to get cozy with Addy. Her professional instincts won out.

"I've been trying to discover the source of some pollutants in the waters of the Chesapeake. I suspect industrial waste dumping, and I want to bring those responsible to justice. Fines aren't enough for those bastards. The fish and crabs, as well as shore birds, suffer terribly from it, not to mention the wetlands."

"Isn't she cute?" Dee-Dee asked, smiling at Addy. "My little environmental do-gooder."

She pinched Liberty's cheek and Liberty peeked uneasily at Addy, who avoided her glance. Aside from Dee-Dee's bodacious boobs dangling tantalizingly before her, Liberty reflected on Chauncey Velasquez's disappearance. His absence suddenly became a giant question mark in her mind, and she vowed to investigate his story thoroughly.

CHAPTER EIGHTEEN

Petey Green's on Drum Point Road didn't have a view of the water like the restaurant Calypso Bay, but the food was pretty good, considering it was in Deale. The small place had a dozen tables or so, if you didn't count the counter-height tables near the bar, and the ambience was indeed much better than that of the Happy Harbor. Karen and Addy sat near the window at the front and perused the menu.

"Wine?" Karen asked.

"That sounds lovely."

Karen ordered the wine, then returned to her menu, occasionally peeping over the top of it at Addy. She was excited to finally spend time with Addy again, yet worried because of what Tommy had said to her. Could the one woman who made her feel like she mattered be a murderer? Surely she was protecting herself, or Tommy, from harm. She couldn't possibly hurt anyone otherwise. But what could the reporter have done to cause such a response?

"The seafood Alfredo is very good," Karen said.

"I'm sure it is, but, oh, the calories."

"You don't need to worry about that." Karen admired Addy's figure. "You're in even better shape than you were in high school."

Addy blushed. "Thank you. So are you."

Karen warmed under Addy's gaze. All the old stirrings rose to the surface, feelings she'd never had for anyone else. She'd been with several women since Addy left, and though she'd had a good time, she missed the connectedness she'd shared with Addy since childhood. Her indiscretion had changed that, but they were still meant for each other. God, she missed Addy so much. But she needed to exonerate her from any involvement in this Vinson situation. Karen didn't want a cloud hanging over her or her brother, and it was better that she be the one to clear them.

Once the waiter took their order and left, Karen lifted her wineglass. "It's great having you back in Deale, Addy. Welcome home."

Addy swallowed hard and could barely speak. "Thank you."

Everything felt so familiar and easy with Karen. The old memories overwhelmed her with heat and emotion. Karen's blue knit shirt highlighted her pale blue eyes, and her black tailored slacks complemented her dark hair. The candlelight flickered softly across her suntanned face, softening the sharp angles of her cheekbones. She was handsome, and Addy was shocked to discover that she wanted Karen very badly.

"I meant to ask you," Karen began, clearing her throat. "How is Scott Vinson's death and finding him on your land affecting you? Are you okay?"

"Fine," Addy said warily. This was not the direction she had expected tonight's conversation to take.

"And Tommy? Is he okay?"

"All the commotion bothered him. You know he doesn't like strangers around. But now that things are getting back to normal, he's better. Why do you ask? Did he say something to make you think otherwise? Maybe I should have a doctor examine him." She leaned back to let the waiter place her plate on the table.

"No, that's not necessary. He was acting a little strange, though, when we talked." Karen tried to gauge Addy's reaction.

"Strange? In what way?"

"I don't know. Like he was hiding something. Tommy has always been able to talk to me, so that surprised me."

Addy's response intrigued and saddened Karen. When Addy was nervous or trying to keep something from her, she always sucked her lower lip. Now, Addy was sucking and biting her lip raw, and she glanced around the room, apparently wanting to get away. Karen had hoped Addy would have an innocent, blank expression.

"What could Tommy possibly be hiding? He never goes anywhere or sees anyone except us."

"My thoughts exactly," Karen said tiredly. "Which is why I decided it might have something to do with you."

"Me?" Addy squeaked. "What are you getting at, Karen? It's just like you to beat around the bush."

"I don't beat around the bush. I've always been straightforward."

"Hah."

"All right. Tommy said you told him not to say anything about Vinson. What didn't you want him to say, Addy?"

The bluntness of Karen's question, and the accusatory tone, rocked Addy against the back of her chair. *Oh, Tommy.* He didn't understand the consequences, how could he? She should have known he would confess to Karen. He was confused and scared, poor thing. What could she say to Karen now? How much of Karen was police officer and how much her lover? Well, *former* lover, anyway. If Dee-Dee was right, and Karen was still in love with her, could she trust Karen?

"Well?" Karen demanded.

Karen's harsh manner irritated her. "What exactly are you implying? That Tommy had something to do with that reporter's death? Don't be absurd."

"It's not Tommy I'm talking about."

Karen's implication finally penetrated Addy's brain. "You

think *I* had something to do with Scott Vinson's death?" She jumped out of her chair. "I can't believe you could think such a thing of me."

"Addy, please—"

"Please nothing."

"Is something wrong with the food?" the waiter asked diffidently.

"Yes. I can't eat it. But I'm sure Officer Kaczarowski has a big enough ego to eat for two."

Addy grabbed her purse and stalked out of the restaurant. She had reached the entrance to the parking lot when Karen called to her to wait, but she didn't stop. At most, it was only a mile to the house, and the evening was pleasantly warm. To think she had planned to let Karen back into her good graces.

❖

Liberty drove her rental car slowly down Masons Beach Road, pondering the pieces of the puzzle she had so far. She hadn't ruled out the cuckoo bird entirely, but new information had come to light regarding Chauncey Velasquez. Cheatham and Grassley's background check had revealed that the guy was in the country illegally and had been for over two years. His disappearance certainly put a new twist on the situation. Could he be involved somehow? Maybe Vinson had uncovered Velasquez's role in an international plot to destroy the Chesapeake Bay watershed.

About to turn onto Parkers Creek, she noticed someone walking along the side of the road. Nearer, she could make out Addy in tan slacks and pale green blouse. She pulled up next to her and lowered the passenger-side window.

"Addy? Everything okay?"

Addy stopped and peered into the car.

"Oh, hi, Liberty. No, I'm not okay, but I will be. Just walking off a little steam, that's all."

"Let me drive you the rest of the way."

Addy got in but stared straight ahead.

"Weren't you out with Officer Kaz—Karen?"

"I was, but she can be the most infuriating, deceptive, callous woman. She was so unbearable, I left the restaurant before we even ate."

"I can't believe anyone would treat you badly. You're such a beautiful woman. If you were mine, I'd treat you the way a woman should be treated."

Liberty was curious as to what had happened but knew Addy and the deputy had a long history. It didn't matter anyhow. This was her opportunity. She massaged the tight muscles in Addy's shoulder, running her fingertips sensuously down her arm.

"*You* have ethics," Addy said, still angry over Karen's accusation. "Karen is heartless."

Liberty's fingers on her skin made her shiver. She had worked up a sweat, and now the air-conditioned car had quickly cooled her off. When Liberty's hand grazed the side of her breast, she trembled. They pulled up to the house and Liberty turned the headlights off. Suddenly, all consideration of Karen evaporated and Addy turned slightly. Ambient light from the moon filtered into the car, but Liberty sat in shadow, her features invisible to her. For a moment, Addy was uneasy.

"You're chilled," Liberty said. "Let me turn off the air."

The car went silent except for the sound of cicadas outside and the pounding of her heart. She had a pretty good idea what was coming next and she didn't care. She wanted Liberty, and she wanted to forget Karen.

"Here, let me warm you up." Liberty wrapped her arm around Addy's shoulders and drew her close. "There now, isn't that better?"

That was definitely *much* better. The chill vanished, and the flames licked at Addy's body like a prairie fire. Within moments, Liberty found her way to Addy's blouse and slowly unbuttoned the top buttons. Her warm hand slipped inside Addy's bra and stroked her heated flesh.

"That feels nice." Addy closed her eyes as Liberty's fingers found her nipple.

"I'll make you feel so good," Liberty murmured, her mouth inches away from Addy's, "you'll forget all about Kazro, Karoz, what's her name."

Liberty covered Addy's mouth with her own and thrust her tongue inside. Addy was hot and welcoming, and Liberty knew she finally had Addy where she wanted her. She shoved Addy's bra aside, tugging roughly on the taut nipple. When Addy moaned in her mouth, Liberty nearly lost control. God, how she loved having women this way. She loved being able to control them, do with them whatever she wished, until they begged her to release their tension. She was good, and women adored her for it. She'd make quick work of this one, then find out just what she and her brother knew about Vinson.

Liberty pressed Addy against the car door, bringing her legs up onto the driver's side. Crawling on top of her, Liberty pushed her bra up the rest of the way and drew a nipple into her mouth.

"Oh, that's *really* good," Addy said.

Liberty sucked and nibbled, running her tongue across the valley between Addy's breasts until she found the other nipple. She rubbed her hand down Addy's abdomen and unzipped her slacks, pushing inside to her panties. She could feel Addy's heat before she even reached the vee between her legs. When her fingers finally found their mark, Addy softly moaned. The sound always triggered the wild animal in Liberty, and she quickly unzipped her own jeans, sliding both their pants down to their knees. As she stroked Addy's wetness, she rode Addy's thigh, gently rocking them both rhythmically.

"Fuck, yeah, that's hot," Liberty said. "You're so ready, I can feel it."

"Yes, please, please do it, make me come." Addy pressed into Liberty, clearly trying to open wider in the confines of the car.

Liberty needed no further encouragement. She continued relentlessly, speeding up, then slowing down, teasing Addy unmercifully, then pulling back.

"God, please, don't stop," Addy said.

Liberty finally settled into a steady stroking while she continued to ride Addy's leg. When Addy released a loud moan, the sound drove Liberty wild, and they came, their bodies shimmering with sweat. Liberty collapsed on top, her heart pounding rapidly against Addy's chest. She wasn't sure if she was hearing her heart or Addy's, but she breathed deeply, trying to slow its beat.

"God, that was good." Liberty sighed.

When Addy didn't respond, Liberty raised up just enough to see her face.

"It was good for you, right?"

"Yes, yes, of course. Sorry."

Addy struggled to sit up and Liberty crawled off her. Addy's mind was elsewhere, probably on Karen, and it ticked her off. She had always kept a woman's attention, and she wasn't about to let that change now.

"You're still thinking about your cop friend." Liberty zipped up her pants. "Mind if I ask what happened?"

Addy struggled to pull her bra back down. "Oh, not much. She thinks I killed that reporter, that's all. Can you believe it? I've never been so outraged."

"That's absurd."

Liberty tried to put the pieces together. Why would Karen think that? Had she discovered some evidence she hadn't shared with her? Was Addy somehow involved more than Liberty had originally figured? Perhaps Tommy had killed the reporter and Addy was protecting him. But maybe Addy instructed Tommy to kill him while she put together some plot of political consequence. Addy had attended Berkeley, a hotbed of revolutionaries and antigovernment sentiment. Maybe while Addy built the bombs,

Tommy was her lookout. But what was Addy protesting? What was her motive? Liberty needed more information, and she'd start gathering it in the morning.

CHAPTER NINETEEN

Karen slouched in her chair, a half-eaten hoagie on her desk. She was completing paperwork on a drunk driver, but her mind wasn't on it. How had her date last night with Addy, which had begun so pleasantly, turned into such a nightmare? Was Addy's indignation warranted, or was she covering something up? Karen shook her head to clear it so she could set aside her personal feelings and examine the facts.

She had only Tommy's word that Addy had asked him to keep quiet about Vinson. What kind of evidence was that? Was Tommy making something up, or was he giving her part of some greater picture? But what was that picture? She massaged her temples, trying to ward off a headache.

"Kaczarowski. In here."

Karen trudged to the chief's office and collapsed in the plastic chair. He motioned for her to close the door, and she gave it a shove.

"I've got McDonald on the speaker phone," he said. "Go ahead, McDonald."

"Officer. I had an interesting conversation last night with Addy Cooper. Would you care to share with me what you've got so far that leads you to suspect that she's involved in the murder of Scott Vinson?"

"She told you about that?" How could Addy confide in this jerk? "What exactly did she say?"

"She said you suspected her in his death. Why do you think that?"

"I don't have anything concrete and I'm not convinced."

"I needn't remind you that even though we're in this together, I'm in charge of this investigation. If you even suspect something, I want to know what it is. Remember, there's more at stake than the reporter here. The Chesapeake may be a target, and we need to stop the terrorists before a catastrophe occurs."

"Addy isn't a terrorist, for God's sake. And neither is her brother."

"Then tell me what's going on so I can help eliminate them from our list of suspects."

Karen hesitated. Liberty didn't understand Tommy and would take what he said out of context, make it into more than it might possibly be. However, what Tommy said was unusual even for him. She had to believe it had some merit. Why else would he say it?

"Sheriff?" Liberty demanded.

"Kaczarowski?" the chief asked.

Karen was annoyed by the federal prerogative, but gave in. She told them of her conversation with Tommy and his revelation about Addy. When she finished, Liberty whistled.

"It doesn't prove anything," Karen said angrily. "Tommy could be playing some sort of game."

"Then why did you mention it to Addy last night? And why did she run out on you when you did?"

Damn it, Addy. Of course, Addy didn't know about McDonald, but it hurt that she had told the FBI agent about their quarrel. Addy would only confide in someone she was growing closer to. Liberty was using Addy to get information, and Karen couldn't stop her.

❖

Frank, Abel, and Clarence waded in hip boots down by the water's edge. Frank had brought along fishing gear in case someone came by and asked what they were doing. They bent over and reached into the water up to their armpits, blindly groping for the camera. Frank had made them scour the tall grass and weeds for nearly two hours, but they had come up empty. The police were sending divers the next morning, and Frank wanted to find the camera before the cops did. They would search their side of the inlet first, and later that night, they'd sneak over to their neighbors' property and inspect the waters there. If they couldn't locate it and the cops did, they were screwed.

"Found something," Abel said.

Frank waded over to where Abel was digging around in the muck. He straightened up and held something covered in mud, then stuck it back in the water to rinse it off. When he raised it again, he held it up for Frank's inspection.

"Shit, it's a density gauge. God damn it, Clarence. Get your ass over here."

Clarence plowed through the water, his arms swinging across his chest as he tried to make his way. "What?"

"You're supposed to be burning this equipment, not dumping it into the inlet, you lame-ass son of a bitch."

"I *was* burning it. I can't help it if the fucking barrel falls over sometimes and stuff falls into the water. What difference does it make?"

"It'll make a shitload of difference if the cops find it, you moron."

"Stop calling me names, Frank." Clarence took a step toward him.

"Not out here." Frank held up his hands defensively. "Those people across the way could be watching. We can take it inside later if you want, Clarence. Right now, we keep hunting."

Even as he spoke, Frank scanned the opposite shore. The rambling Cooper house was mostly hidden behind tall grass and shrubs. He felt reasonably comfortable that no one over there could see them down in the water. Even if they did see them, maybe they would think they were fishing. A flash of reflected sunlight in the tall oak across the way caught his eye, and he stopped what he was doing. Someone *was* watching.

❖

Tommy stared through his binoculars at the figures out in the water, wondering what they were doing. He'd never seen fishermen or crabbers behave that way, but he waited to see what they would catch. The snipe rapidly jabbed his arms into the water, his camouflage clothing at times making him difficult to see. The pelican swooped down into the water to catch whatever lay beneath. And the sandpiper skittered along the shore chasing the waves.

Tommy was getting bored and hungry and was about to turn away from his lookout post when he noticed the snipe standing completely still while the others kept on digging. Sharpening his focus, Tommy gazed into cold gray eyes staring right at him and jumped back in surprise. The stranger looked mean. Tommy brought his binoculars up once more and saw that the man hadn't moved.

"Caw! Caw!"

"Okay, okay," Addy called up to him. "Sorry lunch is late. I had a rough night."

She smiled despite herself. "Rough" was definitely the word she would use for what Liberty had done to her once they got out of the car and into Addy's bedroom. It had been a wild night indeed and she had the bite marks to prove it. In fact, she had to gently sit down on chairs that morning. She felt as though she'd had a strenuous workout at the gym rather than a romantic evening in bed. However, she'd never experienced that kind of sex—certainly not with Maureen. It was all so new and exciting, though a bit intimidating, to keep up with Liberty. She hoped

Liberty had a good time too, but hadn't seen her yet in order to find out.

She put the bologna sandwich in Tommy's bucket, then climbed the tree to the deck where she pulled it up.

"Did you sleep well last night?" she asked.

Tommy nodded.

"Why don't you sit down and eat. Mind if I sit here with you and we can talk?"

"Okay." He tore a corner of his sandwich and stuffed it into his mouth.

"So, did you have a good chat with Karen the other day?" Addy wanted to tread cautiously, but she desperately wanted to know what they had talked about and how much Tommy had given away.

Tommy swallowed. "I guess."

"You like Karen, don't you?"

"Karen's my friend. She remembers my birthday and Christmas and always brings me presents."

Addy knew she shouldn't be surprised, but she was. She had felt especially guilty being away from Grandma Adelaide and Tommy during the holidays. The fact that Karen had taken care of them warmed her. Karen was basically a good person, even if she suspected her falsely. But she had formulated those very suspicions from something Tommy had told her.

"So what all did you talk about?"

Tommy squirmed in his seat. They must have discussed the reporter.

"Did you talk about the man you found, Tommy?"

He nodded. "But I told her you wanted me to keep it a secret, so I didn't say nothing else, Addy."

He seemed so eager to please that she didn't have the heart to scold him. How would she explain the situation to Karen so that she understood? Tommy had discovered the body, and when Addy found out, they'd buried it and decided not to tell anybody.

It didn't sound good even to her own ears. The guy was already dead, so what did it matter?

Addy cringed, barely able to think straight. She wished she had someone to talk to before she went to Karen. A sounding board who could give her advice.

Perhaps Dee-Dee, who had been there for her in the past and hadn't betrayed her secrets. Dee-Dee had helped her through her breakup with Karen and had stayed in touch, letting her know what was going on back home.

Or Liberty, whom she'd just been incredibly intimate with and who seemed to care what happened to her. But she didn't know Liberty well, and what was more important, Liberty didn't know her. What kind of advice could Liberty give her?

God. If only she could just talk openly with Karen. But she was still angry that Karen had assumed she was guilty. How could she? Instead of flinging Tommy's comments into her face, implying she was guilty, Karen should have discussed her assumptions with her calmly. Addy would have explained what happened and Karen should have believed her.

"I'm going into town to do some shopping and I'll bring you some new comic books," Addy said. She cleared Tommy's dishes and returned to the house.

"Oh, Addy," Fern cried as Addy entered the kitchen. "They've arrested Chauncey. What are we going to do?"

CHAPTER TWENTY

Chauncey sat in a tiny room at an equally tiny table shoved against one wall. He fiddled with a tin ashtray, but had no cigarettes to smoke, and nothing to light them with even if he did. They had taken away his Camels, and without them, his nervousness increased. Within moments the door swung open and two large men in suits crowded into the room, along with the deputy, whom he knew.

Behind her he was shocked to see Liberty, a smug look of triumph on her face. He had prided himself on being able to spot a border cop a mile away, but he hadn't suspected his fellow tenant. Ah, well, he was growing old and had let his guard down after two years in the U.S. If they were going to send him back to Mexico, he had put enough money in banks there to live comfortably the rest of his life. He would try to find old friends and family, see if they were still around.

"Would you like a cigarette?" The agent who identified himself as Cheatham shook out one of his Marlboros.

"*Sí*, thank you." Chauncey slid one out and waited for a match.

"Ah, excuse me, but I prefer you not smoke while I'm in the room," Liberty said.

Cheatham gave him a sympathetic smile. Man, being in jail sure wasn't like he remembered the only time the border patrol caught him. It had been his first attempt to enter the country, so he had lacked experience. He had awaited deportation in smoke-filled cells.

"Tell us what you know about the reporter and the radioactive waste in the Chesapeake." Liberty sat in the only other chair in the room, leaving the others to stand.

Chauncey blinked. "I'm sorry. I don't understand what you are talking about."

"Yeah, right, in a pig's ear." Liberty snorted.

"Pig's ear?" Chauncey was becoming more confused. What did a pig and his ear have to do with being in the United States illegally? He had never stolen anything in his life. What would he do with a pig and his ear? While carnitas were his favorite, he had plenty of money and would never have to steal a pig.

"Come on," Liberty snarled. "You killed that guy to cover up whatever you're involved in with the radioactive material. We have a pretty good idea what you're up to. You're going to poison the bay and create chaos and terror on the East Coast. For what purpose? What's the group you belong to, and what's your political beef?"

Chauncey's head swam. She believed he'd killed somebody? And what was this radioactive thing she was talking about? And what was political beef? What were all these animals she accused him of stealing? Were there cows and pigs in this country you were not supposed to eat?

"Miss McDonald, I know nothing about the poor dead man. I already told the police that I was playing horseshoes with old friends down by Mimosa Cove all that day. My friends can tell you. And I do not steal pigs and cows."

"Pigs and cows?" the deputy asked. "What the hell are you talking about?"

"Don't try to change the subject," Liberty said, her face red and angry. "Who's in on this with you? Who's doing the actual dirty-bomb work and what do you want? You'd better tell me now or else it'll be worse for you."

Chauncey looked to each agent in the room and the deputy

as well for some help with all the strange questions Liberty was asking. They were not questions about his being here illegally, but something to do with this dead man they'd found on Miss Addy's land. But he had nothing to do with it.

"My friends can tell you—"

"Forget your stupid friends," Liberty shouted, rising out of her chair and slamming her hands on the table. "They're probably all in it with you. We're going to pick up those so-called friends of yours and haul them in. I don't care how long it takes. We'll break you all one by one until we find out what you're doing and why. What are their names?"

"I don't wish to get anyone into trouble," Chauncey said.

"Screw that." Liberty grabbed him by the arm. "Tell me, or I'll break your arm."

"Sheriff Taylor was there," Chauncey finally confessed. He hoped the sheriff wouldn't get into trouble because of him. He was such a nice man.

Karen dared to peek at Cheatham and Grassley, who were clearly trying to hide their laughter but failing miserably.

"Well, okay, then." Liberty released Chauncey's arm. "You should know that...uh, I'll be talking to the sheriff immediately, and talking to him a lot."

Liberty left the room and Karen followed her.

"I think a woman whose goat went missing filed a complaint the day of Vinson's death," Karen said. "I'll double-check to see if she had any pigs or cows."

"Shut up."

❖

"So Tommy just found him lying there," Dee-Dee said, drawing another draft for Addy. "Big deal. I'm sure Karen will understand. But you need to go tell her and get this mess cleared up. Otherwise, she'll keep thinking you're hiding something, and it'll continue to eat you up inside."

Addy gazed around the bar, making sure no one was paying them any attention. The noisy room made listening in on conversations difficult, but not impossible. "I'm not hiding anything. I just don't want everybody bothering Tommy."

"He's stronger than you think, Addy. The fact that he does come down out of that tree has to prove something. Maybe he's getting better at dealing with life. Maybe he knows that people care for him and will always be around, and that it's okay to trust again."

"I wish I could be certain of that." Addy sighed. "Oh, I don't know. Maybe you're right. I better go tell Karen the whole story. She can probably help keep the media at bay and the questioning to a minimum."

Frank got up from the bar stool and limped to the jukebox in the corner of the room, where he dropped a quarter in and played Patsy Cline's "Crazy." His mind raced at what he'd overheard. So someone *had* been watching them out in the inlet searching for Vinson's camera, and now he knew that same person had probably seen them chasing Vinson almost two weeks ago. But what else had he seen? Why hadn't he told the police or the feds? What was he hiding? Or was he waiting to blackmail them? Could this guy be bought? Did he want in on the action?

He was already planning to take Abel and Clarence over to the Cooper property tonight to search for the camera in the inlet. While they were there, they might visit this guy who lived up in that old oak. If they couldn't buy his silence, maybe it was time to silence him permanently. He returned to his stool and ordered another beer.

"Hey, sweet cheeks," a weather-beaten guy wearing a John Deere cap said. "How's about another Bud?"

"You got it, Billie." Dee-Dee drew a tall one and slid it across the bar.

"We still on for tonight?"

"I'm done by one thirty. I'm counting on it."

"Geez, Dee-Dee," Addy said. "Is there anyone you won't sleep with?"

Dee-Dee laughed. "Probably not. But what else is there to do around here? And it's a helluva lot more fun than going to the movies. A lot cheaper too."

"I thought you'd be done with one-night stands by now." Addy sipped her beer.

"Oh, some are one-nighters, others longer than that. And some I wouldn't mind spending a lot more time with. Like that Liberty. Whooee, she's hotter than a bare ass on Harley chrome."

Addy studied her beer.

"Oh, come on, now," Dee-Dee teased. "It ain't no secret you and Liberty have a little thing goin' on."

Addy snapped her head up. "How do you know?"

"She told me."

"She what?" Addy was appalled that Liberty had been so indiscreet. What they shared was private.

"Hey, it's me," Dee-Dee said. "You don't have to worry about me telling anybody. I could care less that you and her are having a good time. Lord knows there's plenty to go around. And that Liberty sure has enough to share, don't she?"

Addy's face felt hot and she sneaked a peek again to see if anyone was paying attention to them.

"I don't see how that makes it okay for her to kiss and tell."

"Hell, people do it to me all the time. I don't care."

"Yeah, but that's you, Dee-Dee. Everybody knows you sleep around."

"What do you mean by that?" Dee-Dee's voice rose in pitch.

"Oh, come on." Addy laughed at the hurt expression on Dee-Dee's face.

"Are you calling me a whore?" Dee-Dee had her hands on her hips.

The bar quieted down in their corner of the room as a few

heads turned their way. Addy realized Dee-Dee was drawing attention to them, so she tried to cool her down.

"No, Dee-Dee, of course not. But even you have to admit you sleep with a lot of people, men and women."

"Just because I enjoy sex doesn't make me a whore," Dee-Dee snapped. "And having a fucked-up relationship with a deputy sheriff for over six years doesn't make someone a prude. But then again, maybe it does."

The hair on the back of Addy's neck stiffened and she rose from her bar stool. "I am not a prude. I slept with Liberty too, and quite frankly, she was a bit rough. But I suppose you like it that way."

"As a matter of fact, I do." Dee-Dee stepped closer. "And I like it nice and gentle too. The way Karen does it."

The room shrank around Addy, and somewhere in the back of her mind she realized that people had stopped talking. The only sound was someone on television advertising a Toyotathon at the local dealership. She was sick to her stomach and was afraid she might be ill any minute.

"Aw, shit, Addy," Dee-Dee said. "It was a long time ago. Right after you left. It was just a one-time thing, I swear."

Addy stumbled on her way to the door. She wanted to get away—to be anywhere but home, and Deale, and even the state of Maryland. She didn't know where she was going, but she had to go somewhere and think. She couldn't seem to think.

CHAPTER TWENTY-ONE

Each time Addy reached the end of a street, she turned left or right, whichever one took her away from Deale. At times she pulled over in indecision, trying to clear her mind, and then drove on. She would have given anything for her grandmother. Grandma Adelaide was tough and no-nonsense when it came to affairs of the heart. She would have told Addy that life was hard and how you dealt with it made you stronger. Then she would have dragged Addy out of her depression and cooked her some macaroni and cheese.

When Masons Beach dead-ended, she pulled over and got out. Lights along the shoreline twinkled in the ink black sky, and a warm breeze blew in off the ocean. She walked along the sand for a long time and reflected on her life—where she'd been and where she was going. Most of her choices had been by accident. Aside from actually choosing to go to Berkeley, she had lost her parents, been a victim of Karen's infidelity, and merely agreed when Maureen insisted that they move in together and that she accept the first job offer that came along.

And now she was back in Deale, a place that evoked such mixed emotions. She loved Tommy dearly and would do anything for him, but once again her life had been decided for her. He was her responsibility and depended entirely upon her, but what about her happiness? Maureen had been a mistake, she could see that now. Addy had run away from Deale, or rather from Karen, and into the arms of someone she didn't love. Since returning to Deale, she had been unwillingly drawn back to Karen, both physically and emotionally. But could she trust herself, trust her choices anymore? And what was Liberty to her? Who was she and how did she feel about Addy?

All the questions overwhelmed her and she began to run down the beach. She wanted to keep going until she collapsed from exhaustion. Maybe then her mind would be still and she could sleep.

❖

"Shh," Frank whispered. "You sound like a Humvee out on maneuvers."

"I can't see a damn thing," Clarence said.

"Try opening your eyes."

They cautiously stepped through the dense underbrush along the Cooper side of the inlet. They had driven to within a mile of the house, then hiked along the shore until they could make out the house lights. They'd brought a net and wading boots and sat on stumps near the dock to put their waders on.

"Forget hunting on land, the cops have already done that. Focus on the water. Here." Frank handed Abel the net. "Start over there and spread out. Let me know the minute you find anything."

They reached into the water and blindly searched the inlet bed for the reporter's camera. The only sound was the soft swish of water as it moved against their boots and arms. But after an hour, they had only unearthed rocks and shells and bits of driftwood. Frank was becoming annoyed, and he worried that at any time someone would come out to see what they were up to.

"There's nothing here, Frank," Abel whispered. "Maybe it's out in deeper water. He swam across from our side to here. He could've lost it anywhere."

Clarence said, "We'll never find it."

"If he had it in the first place."

Frank scanned the tree house behind them and saw the impressive structure clearly for the first time. Maybe the guy who lived there was spying on them right now. If he wasn't, then he had to be asleep. The woman said he never left. The guy must be crazy or something, which could only work in their favor. No way would anyone believe a Section 8 guy over a Gulf War vet. But the camera bothered him. The cops weren't even sure it existed, but they must have some reason to send out divers. *If there was a camera, God knows what was on it.* Maybe that guy up there would know. Maybe he had the camera already and was waiting to blackmail them even now.

"Follow me." Frank started wading back to shore and toward the oak.

"Are you nuts?" Clarence rasped. "Where are you going?"

"Up there." Frank pointed at the tree.

"Frank." Abel pulled him aside. "We gotta get outta here before someone asks us what we're doing. Let's go home, there ain't no camera."

"We have to be sure. And that guy up there can probably tell us one way or the other."

Clarence and Abel hung back as Frank limped to the base of the tree. But when Frank motioned them onward, they followed. Once at the top, Frank tried the door but it was locked.

"Hey, little buddy. We want to talk with you about the reporter. I'll bet you can see real good up here, can't you? Did you notice if he had a camera with him?"

There was nothing except the sounds of the night. Frank tried the doorknob again with no luck.

"Shit," Frank said. "Give me something to open this with, Abel."

"I don't have anything."

"What the fuck," Clarence said. "I didn't know we were supposed to bring lock picks with us on this expedition."

"You should always be prepared," Frank growled.

"Then why didn't you bring something? You're the Boy Scout of the family." Clarence began to laugh at his own joke, his horsey snort getting louder.

"Quiet, asshole." Frank glared at Clarence. He put his weight against the door and tried as quietly as possible to force it open. But the door was solid and immovable. "Damn, who made this door?" He stepped back and ran shoulder-first into it, and it still wouldn't budge.

"What's the kid's name again?" Frank asked.

"Papers said it was Tommy Cooper," Abel said. "He and his sister live here. Well, she lives down there. Why do you think he lives up here, Frank?"

Frank stared at him. In a singsong voice he repeated Abel's question. "'Why do you think he lives up here, Frank?' How the fuck would I know? Shut up and help me get the goddamn door open, will ya?"

All three of them stepped as far from the door as they could. Turning sideways and tilting their shoulders down, they charged. As they braced for impact, the door opened wide and they crashed into the house. Frank fell into the table, knocking comic books and a chair over, but he quickly jumped to his feet and crouched in a defensive posture.

The boy stared wide-eyed at them, like he was half asleep.

"We ain't gonna hurt you, kid," Abel said.

"Speak for yourself," Clarence muttered.

"Shut up." This wasn't exactly a kid, but Frank was confident he could take him even without Clarence and Abel's help. Pretty much like the reporter.

"Your name's Tommy, right?"

Tommy nodded. The one in army clothes, the one that reminded him of a snipe, seemed to be the boss. Tommy wondered what they wanted. They sure had been noisy. He had tried to call Addy when he first heard them, but she didn't answer, so he decided to open the door before they got any louder. They made him nervous, and he began to flap his wings, like he always did when he wanted to fly away.

"See, I know a lot about you already, like your name," the snipe said. "I also know that you came down out of this tree and found that guy by the water."

"Caw! Caw!"

"Shut up!" the one that looked like a pelican yelled.

"Quiet!" The snipe looked like he hated the pelican.

"What the fuck's up with the bird call?" the sandpiper asked.

"The kid's got a screw loose, don't sweat it." The snipe moved slowly toward Tommy, holding out his hands. "It's okay. I'm not going to say anything about it to anyone, as long as you don't either. What I want to know is, did you see us go after him?"

Tommy nodded again.

"Holy shit, let's get rid of him now," the big pelican said.

"The kid thinks he's a bird. Do you think anybody would believe anything he says?" The snipe stared at Tommy again. "Did you tell anybody you saw us?"

Tommy shook his head.

"Good boy," he said. "Now you just keep quiet about that and everything will be okay. We wouldn't want to hurt you or your sister, would we, you guys?"

The other two shook their heads.

"One more thing, Tommy. Did you see if the guy had a camera with him? You know, a little box that takes pictures. Did you see one?"

Tommy didn't say anything. He wasn't supposed to lie. His grandma had told him that. He didn't see many people, so he never needed to. But he felt like he shouldn't tell them about the camera he'd found and hid under his bed. He'd give it to Karen instead. She'd be sure the camera went to the right person.

"Tommy, do you know what a camera is?" the snipe kept saying.

"Yes, but I don't know how to make one work."

"That's good, that's okay," the snipe said, like he was trying to be nice. "But the man lost his, and we just want to find it. Did you find his camera?"

"There's a car coming down the road," the sandpiper whispered.

"Let's go." The pelican hurried to the door and went out on the deck.

"Did you find his camera?" the snipe said again.

He grabbed Tommy by the arm, and that scared him even more.

"Caw! Caw!"

"To hell with that lunatic, Frank. Let's get outta here." Clarence scrambled down the tree but Abel hesitated at the rung.

"Come on, Frank," he pleaded.

Frank stared at Tommy, trying to decipher if he knew anything about the camera. But Tommy broke loose from his grasp and hopped onto his bed, flapping his arms and cawing at the ceiling. No way was that kid going to convince anyone they had anything to do with Vinson's death, even if he witnessed them doing it. Who would believe a fruitcake like that? But if he had the camera, that was another thing.

"Keep your mouth shut, kid. If you say anything to anybody, I'll come after you—and your sister."

Tommy quieted.

"That's right. Now I've got your attention, don't I?" Frank grinned. "Keep it to yourself that we were here and everything will be fine."

Frank edged his way out the door, keeping his eyes on Tommy's. When he reached the ladder, he finally looked away and left.

Tommy sat on his bed and stared out the door. His heart beat fast, and he didn't understand what had happened and what it all meant. He was scared and didn't know what to do. He'd never had strangers in his house before, except maybe that Liberty lady. She scared him too.

The snipe wanted the camera, and he knew he better get rid of it before he and the others came back. If the bad men took the camera, they would never give it back to the crane. But the crane was dead. Who did it belong to now? He didn't know, but he didn't want the camera in his house anymore.

CHAPTER TWENTY-TWO

Addy sat at the picnic table as the police divers swam around the inlet, their black neoprene heads occasionally bobbing to the surface like the seals along the California coast. She sipped a cup of coffee and tried to clear her clouded brain from her restless night. Three cups of coffee later, the caffeine still hadn't helped.

Karen stood by the spot where the reporter was found, her short sleeves revealing the tanned muscles of her arms. She was stunning in the morning light, her bronzed skin gleaming. Addy's body stirred at the sight, but when she recalled Dee-Dee's comment, she immediately squelched the sensation.

She supposed she couldn't begrudge Karen companionship all these years. But that she had slept with Dee-Dee, her best friend, really hurt. Anonymous sex was one thing, but this was something else.

Surprised to see Karen heading straight for her, she braced for the encounter. Karen suspected her of murder.

"Good morning." Karen sat down.

"Officer," Addy said stiffly.

Karen sighed loudly.

"They've been out there for hours," Addy said. "Haven't they found anything to tie me to the murder yet? Addy Cooper, with the candlestick, in the library?"

"This isn't a game, Addy. A man is dead."

"I know that. You haven't let me forget it. Why don't you search my house? Surely you'll find some blunt object I used as the murder weapon. Of course, my fingerprints are all over everything, so it'll be difficult to narrow your choices. Hell, I'll make it easy on you and just confess. You can haul me away in handcuffs, get your picture in the paper and all that."

"Dammit, Addy. Why don't you just tell me what's going on? We've got to know what Tommy is talking about. Why are you so damn stubborn?"

"Because…" Addy struggled to think of a reply, but she was too tired—of fighting Karen, of holding on to the anger she'd felt for years. She released a long breath and gave in, trying to say what she felt. "I don't know. I was shocked that you would think me capable of such a thing. You know me better than that."

"Oh, Addy." Karen moved to the opposite side of the picnic table and gazed into her eyes. "I want to help you and Tommy. But I can't if you don't trust me."

Trust. That's really what it boiled down to. The tenderness in Karen's eyes made Addy want to believe her. In the end, Karen was probably the only one she *could* trust.

"Here you are," Liberty said, strolling up. She sat down right next to Addy. "I've been looking all over for you. Want to go for a drive? Maybe up to Baltimore for the day. The aquarium has a fantastic gallery that traces the water cycle from a freshwater pond through a tidal marsh, onto a coastal beach, and out into the Atlantic. It's a wonderful place to study aquatic environments. Sound good?"

Liberty smiled seductively and ran a finger up Addy's arm, which nauseated and angered Karen. She couldn't believe the smarmy tactics the agent had used to delude Addy. Besides, what kind of date was going to an aquarium? As if Addy hadn't been around the sea all her life.

"Uh, yeah, sure," Addy said slowly. "Let me go change. It'll only take five minutes."

Liberty's eyes were fixed on Addy's ass as she walked away. That really pissed Karen off, and the heat rose to her face.

"I snuck up the tree last night and talked to Tommy again," Liberty informed her. "Man, was he uptight. I tried to get any information I could about Vinson's camera, and this time I really thought he was going to flip out. Something about that camera has him all atwitter."

"I told you to leave him alone. He doesn't know what he's talking about."

"Despite the bird act, I think he does know something. His sister killed the guy, and he's covering up for her."

Karen laughed. "Now you're the crazy one. What possible motive would Addy have for killing Vinson? And how in the world does that tie in with the radioactive waste you think he was investigating?"

"I was hoping you'd ask." Liberty glanced at the house and lowered her voice. "Seems like Ms. Cooper moved home when her former employer, a Russian import/export businessman, was arrested and his company shut down. We traced some of what he was importing directly to the Russian government. I don't have to tell you how very little control the Russians have over their nuclear arsenal. It's common knowledge within the department, and all over the newspapers. They'd sell it to anyone for a few bucks and some exported American goods. Think about it."

Karen stared at her. "And you think Addy was involved?"

"It's pretty coincidental, don't you think?" Liberty folded her arms across her chest and smiled. "She had access to God-knows-what was coming and going in that organization. We checked out her financial situation. It always boils down to money, doesn't it? Aside from a house in Oakland and this place here, financially she's in pretty dire straits. She's got some serious credit-card debt, a mortgage back in California, and high taxes on this property. And she's got no means to support herself, aside from a couple of tenants. She was selling nuclear material to some questionable people, and when Vinson found out, she got rid of him."

"You have got to be kidding. There's no way in hell Addy would do such a thing. She's as American as anybody else."

"She went to Berkeley," Liberty said, as though that explained it all. "Cheatham and Grassley have been doing some digging. It seems Ms. Cooper protested our invasion of Iraq by participating in a sit-in that turned violent. Let's suppose she didn't do anything intentionally but just needed money. Soon things got out of control and she couldn't find her way out of the mess she was in. That happens all the time. Maybe she didn't mean to hurt him, but she was desperate, and before she knew it, he was dead. I don't have to go for premeditation on the murder. But the nuclear stuff is another thing. She's fucked with the environment, and nobody gets a break from me. I'll nail her pretty ass to the wall for hurting animals, so help me God."

"Leave Addy's ass out of it."

Liberty grinned. "Ah, you see? You've got a thing for her and it blinds you to what she's capable of. I don't blame you. She's a great piece of ass, no doubt about it."

Karen jumped up and grabbed Liberty by her shirt front.

"Karen? What's going on?" Addy let the screen door slam behind her as she gazed curiously at the two women. They didn't like each other, that was obvious. Were they fighting over her again? She hated to admit that she liked the idea, especially Karen's jealousy, but even so, she didn't want things to get ugly.

"Nothing." Liberty removed Karen's hands from her shirt. "Just a friendly disagreement. You ready to go?"

Addy nodded, caught between them.

"I hope you find what you're searching for," Liberty said to Karen. "It would be nice to know the bad guys were behind bars and the world was safe again."

Addy glanced over her shoulder as she followed Liberty to the car. She wanted so much to run to Karen, to hold her and be held. For the life of her, she didn't know why she couldn't.

❖

Tommy pulled the nylon bag out from under his bed and removed the camera. He needed to get rid of it as soon as he could. All the scary people coming to his house to ask him about it upset him. But where could he put it so no one could find it? The police were always searching the land and water, and it wouldn't be a good idea for them to find it here. And while he walked all over the farm at night, he never once left the property. Suddenly, he knew just the place.

The painters left when the sun went down, and Addy hadn't come back yet with that Liberty lady he didn't like. He hoped Addy wasn't in trouble. He saw through his window that Mrs. Bush and Chauncey were at the dining room table, playing cards. Now was the best time to get it out of his house. As he got up from the floor, the camera strap caught on a bedspring under the mattress and jerked out of his hands. The camera fell to the floor, making the back pop open, and several parts scattered around the room. Scooping it all off the floor, Tommy closed it and hoped it wasn't broken.

He put the camera strap around his neck and scrambled down the tree to the back porch. Quietly he opened the screen door, pausing only when its hinges creaked. The television was on inside and no one bothered to come see who was there. He sneaked into the house and peeped through the kitchen and into the dining room, where Mrs. Bush and Chauncey kept their eyes on their cards.

"Full house," Mrs. Bush announced.

"*Mierda*," Chauncey said.

Chauncey bent to remove a sock. What kind of game could they be playing? His shoes and one other sock were already scattered across the dining room floor.

"A few more hands ought to do it," Mrs. Bush sang out, like she was excited.

Tommy tiptoed down the hallway and reached the stairs. He was about to keep going to his grandma's room when a key turning in the front door lock alerted him that Addy was home.

He ran as quietly as he could up the stairs and hid around the corner, peeking down to the door below.

"Let's go to my room." Liberty had her arms wrapped around Addy's waist.

"Shh," Addy said. "They'll hear you."

"They're going to hear more than that if they come upstairs."

She jerked Addy's hand, and Tommy hurried down the hall into Addy's bedroom. He closed the door and waited as they giggled on their way to Liberty's bedroom. When he heard her door close, he sneaked back downstairs to his grandma's closet and dug around inside for a place to hide the camera. First he tried a shoe box that wasn't wide enough, then a plastic tub that wasn't deep enough. Finding a box full of photo albums on the shelf, he put the camera on top, replaced the lid, then crept back to the door. He opened it a crack and, seeing no one in the hallway, hurried to the kitchen and out the door without a sound.

❖

Addy lay awake, her body once again sated but sore. Liberty sprawled across the bed, snoring softly into her pillow. Her left arm was flung haphazardly across Addy's stomach, and Addy shifted to lessen its dead weight. Despite her body's tranquil state, her mind wouldn't be still. She had all but decided to tell Karen what had happened that night with Tommy. Better to tell her than some stranger.

But what would happen after she divulged the information? Presumably Karen would have to report it to her superiors, who would have to investigate further. Could she shield Tommy from the onslaught of questions? Would anyone believe that Tommy had come down from his tree house and simply found a body?

She gazed at Liberty asleep and wondered what she was dreaming about or, more importantly, what she was thinking when they made love. The sexual gymnastics were becoming a bit tiring, and she wished they could slow things down. Addy preferred her sex to be gentler, softer, more romantic. Liberty seemed to be trying to impress her more than satisfy her, which wasn't what she wanted. She had run away to California in search of something and someone new, to find only empty promises.

Now, back where she had started from, she had believed she might find meaning in a relationship with Liberty. But that too was proving futile. Only with Karen had she found the happiness she desired—Karen, whom she trusted and confided in, and who had always defended her. She had to trust Karen to believe her, which was what mattered most. But could she?

Chapter Twenty-three

Addy asked Karen to meet her at Owings Beach the next afternoon, then arrived early to clear her mind. She strolled along the shore, letting the incoming tide wash over her feet before it receded. The cool water on her bare skin and the sound of the waves soothed her. During her childhood, she had spent endless days searching the coast for pieces of washed-up treasure that she kept in a cigar box.

She had first met Karen here on a scorching summer's day, when everyone who could had escaped the city to cool off. Addy was focused on the sand, searching for seashells and anything else of interest to add to her collection. The beach was crowded and she hadn't had much success, so she had extended her coverage beyond her usual sandy stretch. Late in the afternoon when she walked to the edge of the tall grass and weeds that marked the end of the swimming area, she had discovered a lone girl sitting on a large rock just beyond the sandy area, probing the sandy bottom with a stick, trying to find her own riches.

A car door slammed, and Karen stepped out of the parking area and on to the beach. Except for her black shoes and dark coloring, she blended seamlessly with the sand, like a moving mirage. Addy gazed toward the ocean, intensely happy. But at the same time, the old pain reasserted itself. Her sense of loss nearly overwhelmed her, and she wanted to rage at an unfair world.

"Hi," Karen said, her voice almost snatched away by the wind.

Addy smiled wanly. "Thank you for coming."

"Sure. Do you want to walk?"

Karen's dark hair whipped back and forth across her face as she stood with her hands shoved deep into her pockets. Her air of quiet self-confidence had always made Addy feel somehow stronger.

They didn't speak as they walked on the damp sand near the water's edge. Even though Addy had planned what she wanted to say, now she didn't know where to begin. After a few minutes, though, she began to relax as she listened to the waves and the call of the seagulls.

"Remember the night of our junior year when they had that bonfire here on the beach?" she asked.

Karen pointed to a small cove up ahead. "It was there. You, me, Dee-Dee, and whoever she was with at the time, the Turner twins and their girlfriends. You wore that green sleeveless T-shirt I always liked."

"You remember that?" Addy warmed to the memory.

"I've never forgotten a single minute of being with you. Meeting you over there when we were kids," Karen pointed to the rock, "or the first time we kissed, or the first time we made love."

Addy's eyes filled. She had never been happier, never been so loved and wanted. If only she could feel that way again.

"And I've never forgotten the *last* time we made love," Karen said softly.

Addy gazed up at her. Karen's expression, filled with such pain and sorrow, made her grasp Karen's arm. They stopped walking and Karen gazed into her eyes.

"I'm so sorry about Miss Wilson. I was such a fool, and I never meant to hurt you. I wish I could take it all back, but I guess it's too late."

Addy still grasped Karen's forearm, and she slowly stroked it with her thumb.

"It's never too late to say you're sorry." Addy wanted to say more, but part of her still held back. She needed to get this thing with Tommy off her chest, but where to begin?

"I *am* sorry." Karen placed her hand on Addy's. "Please say you forgive me and that we can move on. I've waited a very long time to hear you say it."

The warmth of Karen's hand made Addy tingle inside. Whenever Karen touched her, Addy's willpower vanished.

"I'm tired of being angry at you. It was a long time ago and we were both so young." Finally, she said, "I forgive you." The words emerged as a whisper and surprised her. A heavy weight lifted from her shoulders, and she felt as though she could float on a gust of wind like the seagulls riding the airstream above.

She began to walk again, but separating from Karen chilled her. She needed to let go of one last thing.

"I need to tell you about that night."

Karen listened to Addy's story as open-mindedly as she could. Addy was obviously telling the truth. She wouldn't lie, and the details of the story were simply too bizarre to invent. When Addy finished, Karen remained silent, trying to process what she had heard.

Tommy had to be innocent, but who else but them would believe that? What exactly did he know about the death of Scott Vinson? Had he seen anyone nearby before the murder, and if so, would she be able to extricate that information from him?

"You don't believe me," Addy said softly.

Karen stopped walking and faced her. "That's not true. I don't for one minute suspect you or Tommy."

Unable to stand, Addy flung herself into Karen's arms and sobbed. She cried until she was spent, then rested in Karen's embrace. The wind and the waves crashed around them, safe together.

"You know I have to tell the sheriff everything you've told me."

Addy tensed, then let go. She couldn't deny what she'd said, and the inevitable consequences of the truth had to play out. She nodded.

"Please, help me take care of Tommy. He can't take the pressure of being questioned, and I could lose him forever." She had been Tommy's guardian such a short time and was already failing. Her grandmother would never have let things get so far out of hand. Without Karen, Addy would surely lose control entirely.

"I'll do everything possible to help him. But the detectives handling the case will definitely want to talk to him. It might be best to have a psychiatrist available."

Addy couldn't hope for anything better, but she still worried. She clung to Karen, willing her strength to infuse her.

Karen gazed out at the ocean, pondering Addy's story. She had denied knowing anything about the crime, and this Johnny-come-lately revelation would go hard on her. But Tommy really worried her. Others might view him as unstable and potentially capable of a crime, and Addy's apparent cover-up could make her an accomplice. Would she be able to safeguard either of them?

"I guess we should be getting back," Addy murmured.

Karen nodded, but was reluctant to release her. She closed her eyes and allowed the sensation of Addy in her arms to wash over her. All too soon, Addy pulled away, and Karen opened her eyes to the wind.

As it loosened a strand of hair from Addy's barrette at the base of her neck, Karen placed her fingertips on the strand and couldn't let go. This was Addy, standing before her as she had dreamed of for so long. It was time to clear the past of all the cobwebs. Addy had forgiven her, and now she could forgive herself. Now that the moment was here, she wanted it to last forever. She brushed Addy's cheek and let her fingers rest under her chin. Tilting Addy's face upward, she kissed the soft lips that she had fantasized about for so many years.

Addy leaned forward, the heat of Karen's body drawing her like a magnet. She ached for her touch, ached to lie alongside her as they had during simpler times. They were different people now, but the passion that Addy had believed was long gone rushed to the surface in a groundswell of need. The gentle kiss quickly changed to open mouths and furtive tongues, searching for the truth of each other's emotions.

She teased Karen's lips with her tongue, then traced a flickering path inside her mouth until she was lost in the heat and the thrill of the familiar. She knew Karen's body and needs as well as her own, and she realized she had finally found what she was seeking—herself. Karen was as much a part of her as Tommy, and had been in her life almost as long. The two of them were her home.

When the intensity abated, Karen stepped back and held her at arm's length. "You need to go home, and I need to…" Her voice was rough.

"I know." Addy pressed her fingers to Karen's lips. "You need to do what you have to. I understand."

Holding hands, they walked slowly back to the parking lot. Karen helped her into her car, then closed the door. Addy knew Karen would head immediately for the station.

Chapter Twenty-four

Addy stepped out of the shower and toweled off, feeling much better. The hot water had rinsed off the sea salt and erased her troubled mind. She put on clean clothes and brushed her hair back into a ponytail. Tossing her towel into her laundry basket, she frowned at the overflowing basket, but as she picked it up she felt a twinge in her back.

"Oh." She placed a hand near the base of her spine.

"Need a hand?"

Liberty, casually propped against the door frame, resembled the Cheshire cat.

"Laundry day. But thanks anyway."

Liberty entered the bedroom and wrapped her arms around Addy, pulling her close. "Why do laundry when I'm just going to get you all dirty again?" She nuzzled Addy's neck and nipped playfully along her jawline.

"Because I hate doing laundry, so I have tons of it. At some point I have to give in." Addy struggled to escape Liberty's embrace.

"Mmm, sure I can't distract you? We could find a better way to spend time."

"I've got too much housework today."

"Your house is always spotless," Liberty mumbled in her ear, sucking the lobe gently, "so housecleaning is out. Chauncey takes care of the garden, and Fern loves to cook. What else could we find to do?"

Her mouth traveled farther down Addy's throat to the open collar, where her tongue began a sensuous dance.

"Liberty, I really am busy today."

"For instance?"

"Well, I want to move my things downstairs to my grandmother's old room. Enough time has passed, and if I can fix this room up, I can rent it too." Addy gently pushed Liberty away before she changed her mind.

Liberty sighed. "Oh, okay. At least let me help you carry the heavy stuff. Where do you want to start?"

"Thanks, I appreciate it. I don't have much up here, just what's in the bathroom and closet. If you could take the clothes on hangers, that would be great. I'll deal with the bathroom."

Liberty had carried two loads of clothes downstairs and was back in the bedroom by the time Addy had filled a box with her toiletries.

"What about the rest of these things in the closet?"

"They go too," Addy called from the bathroom, then joined her in the closet.

Liberty lifted the largest box down first. "Geez, what've you got in here, rocks?"

"Those are old photo albums. You can put them in the storage room. I don't look at them very often."

"If there are pictures of you in here, I wouldn't mind seeing them. Especially one of you naked." Liberty smiled and waggled her eyebrows.

"Very amusing, but no. No naked pictures. I'll show them to you on the next boring rainy day."

Liberty hefted the box to rest against her stomach and carried it down the stairs. Addy followed and was almost to her grandmother's room when the doorbell rang.

"Hi." Karen stood at the door, her eyes sparkling in the sunlight.

"Hi," Addy said thickly. The mere sight of Karen made her nervous system go haywire.

"We need to talk," Karen whispered. "I don't want to upset Tommy, but I believe he knows more than he's let on. Please, Addy, before it's too late."

"I understand. It's time to put this behind us."

"Yes," Karen said. Addy was beautiful, her damp hair pulled back just like it always was after a shower. Addy always showered after they made love, and then Karen would drag her back to bed and start all over again.

"Well, good morning, Officer." Liberty peered over Addy's shoulder. "What brings you out here?"

The knot in Karen's stomach tightened. She resented the fact that Liberty and Addy lived together, even if only as landlord and tenant. Liberty insinuated that it was more than that, and if the rumors were true, it was. She noticed the two of them holding boxes.

"Moving out, Ms. McDonald?"

"Just moving some things into Addy's room," Liberty replied, and winked.

Karen narrowed her eyes and clenched her fists.

"Why don't you come in?" Addy backed up to let Karen through the door. She kept herself between the two women as they took their measure of each other.

"I remember that box," Karen said wistfully as she sat on the sofa. "I'm so glad you kept it."

"You hated having your picture taken."

"I can see why," Liberty interjected.

"You know, McDonald—"

"Liberty, would you excuse us for a minute? I need to talk to the deputy."

"Not a problem." Liberty smiled at her. "After I put this box in the storage room, what can I do?"

"How about taking some more boxes from my grandmother's closet down to storage. Thanks."

When Liberty had gone, Karen glared at Addy. "What's she doing with all that stuff?"

After she explained, Karen pressed. "Is she moving in with you?"

Addy sighed. "I thought we were going to talk about Tommy."

"All right. Let's go talk to him."

Addy shivered, transported to that night, which seemed like a dream or, rather, a nightmare. She would never forget the sights and smells. She tried to gauge Karen's feelings.

"I'll take you up to see him, but do you believe that neither Tommy nor I had anything to do with this?"

"I—" Karen began.

"I for one don't believe that."

They swiveled to see Liberty standing in the hallway, a Nikon camera dangling from her outstretched hand.

❖

"You lied to me. Again!" Addy sobbed. Wearing handcuffs, she stumbled on her way to the squad car parked in front of the house. When Karen caught her and prevented her fall, she jerked her arm away as though burned.

"Addy, I couldn't say anything about Liberty. She was undercover. It would be a federal offense to tell you." Karen followed her, miserable. How in the hell had that camera come to be in Addy's possession? She despised Liberty, but knew she would never plant it. She had found it and would delight in showing it off—even if only to gloat within the department.

"Watch your head." Karen helped her into the car.

"Get your hands off me."

"Addy!" Fern ran to the window of the patrol car, wheezing from her ten-yard sprint. "Don't worry about Tommy. Mr. Velasquez and I will look out for him. Even if you get life, we'll be here. You know, this reminds me of a book I read once. It was called *Murder Finds a Mistress*. It was about this woman who—"

"Thank you, Mrs. Bush." Addy sniffed. "But I fully intend to be vindicated and home soon."

"Do you have a lawyer?"

Addy paused. "Well, no."

Fern gazed at her pityingly. "Like I said, don't worry about Tommy. We'll take good care of him. They usually don't put convicted murderers in with other prisoners, so you'll have a cell all to yourself. Won't that be nice? I'll crochet a little coverlet for you—something with flowers and birds on it, to brighten things up."

"Thanks."

Karen climbed into the seat beside her, and the officer up front steered the car down Parkers Creek Drive. Addy kept her head turned toward the window so she could avoid looking at Karen. She was stunned that Liberty was an FBI agent. Liberty had used her, and she wondered if the sex was just one of the perks of the job.

Addy was disgusted with everyone, but even more so with herself. She had trusted an ex-lover and a current lover, and they had both screwed her.

❖

Addy wiped the ink from her fingertips as a deputy finished taking her picture. Then he led her to a cell where he informed her she would stay for a while. The small bland room contained only the basics, and on the wall someone had scrawled several opinions. *"Fascist pigs!" "I'm innocent." "This cell would look so much better in pale aquas and mint greens."*

In the cell across the way, a large woman groaned as she rolled off the side of her cot and landed on her butt with a thump.

"Holy mother of God," the woman whined.

"Are you all right?"

The bleached blonde with streaked mascara seemed to have a hard time focusing on Addy. Her clothes were disheveled and unkempt, her hair sticking up in all directions.

"Who the hell are you?" she asked.

Embarrassed to give her name to the stranger or to explain why she was there, Addy tried to come up with an answer.

"Honey, don't hurt yourself. It ain't a complicated question." The woman stopped weaving and moaned again. This time she scrambled to her knees and crawled to the toilet, where she immediately emptied the contents of her stomach.

Addy felt her own stomach roil and turned away. She was miserable and lonely, and she worried about Tommy. She needed to find out what was going on, but no one would tell her.

"Ah, that feels better." The blonde belched, then grinned at Addy. "Tied one on last night. Don't remember a thing."

Addy smiled wanly. If this was her companion during her stay in the county jail, she would confess to the murder right now. A door opening down the hall drew her attention. Karen strode toward her, and Addy turned her back on her.

Karen sighed. "Addy, if I'm going to help you, you need to talk to me."

Addy whirled around. "I *did* talk to you, and look what it got me."

"I didn't know you had hidden Vinson's camera in your house."

"I *told* you I didn't know anything about it. I have no idea how it got there. If you don't believe me, we don't have anything to discuss."

"There has to be some plausible reason why it was there. The judge isn't going to believe you haven't got a clue about it."

"That's his problem. I can't explain something I don't understand."

"If that's true, only Fern, Chauncey, or Tommy could have put it there."

"Tommy hasn't set foot in the house since he was a child."

"You don't know that. You never thought he came down from the tree until Vinson. If it isn't Tommy, who would you pick as the culprit? Fern or Chauncey?"

Addy struggled to answer. Neither her brother nor her tenants were capable of the crime. It simply didn't make sense. Besides, Fern and Chauncey had irrefutable alibis. Only she and Tommy were unaccounted for. She still refused to believe Tommy had done anything. But how did that camera get in her grandmother's closet?

"I don't know."

Karen sighed again. "In the morning you'll see the judge. He'll set bail and the process will begin."

Chapter Twenty-five

A ddy ate her greasy fried chicken and imitation mashed potatoes with peas. She washed them down with coffee, but was unable to taste anything. Dull and defeated, she lacked the energy and the will to think, so she let her mind wander until Fern and Chauncey stopped in front of her cell. A deputy lingered a short distance away.

"*Madre de Dios*. What is this country coming to that it must put in prison someone like you, Miss Addy?"

"This is jail, Mr. Velasquez, not prison," Fern said. "Addy doesn't go to prison until she is convicted of the crime. Jail is merely a temporary condition."

Fern smiled sweetly at Addy, as though the distinction should comfort her.

"I've been able to extricate Mr. Velasquez from *his* temporary confinement until the issue of his immigration comes up for consideration. My nephew is a lawyer and thinks he can help him. Oh, by the way, I baked you banana nut bread." Fern held the loaf out for Addy's inspection, then muttered, "Be sure to eat it while it's fresh."

Their visit rejuvenated Addy. "Thank you both so much for coming to see me. How's Tommy taking it?"

Fern frowned. "Well, he's been a little upset, Addy. He keeps asking for you, wondering where you are."

"Poor Tommy. What will become of him?"

"Don't you go worrying about that," Fern said. "I have plenty of money. Tommy is like my own. Why, in some respects, he reminds me of my third husband—God rest his soul. A little touched in the head, but sweet as apple pie."

"Thank you, Miss Bush." Addy grasped her hand. "I can never repay you for your kindness."

The door down the hall opened and Liberty headed their way. "Please excuse us," she said. "I need to speak to Addy alone."

"Addy, don't talk to her without your lawyer," Fern said, letting go of Addy's hand. "She's shifty and untruthful. I didn't like her from the start."

"Thank you, Fern, but I'll be all right. You'd better leave now. Please let me know how Tommy is doing."

Liberty smiled. "Good evening to you, Miss Bush, Mr. Velasquez."

"Well, I never." Fern cast a disdainful glance at Liberty. "I have packed up your belongings, Miss McDonald, and deposited them in the front hall. You are no longer welcome in our home." She took Chauncey's arm in hers and stomped out.

Addy stared at her. "Are you here to gloat, Liberty, or were you looking for some recreational sex?"

"Tell her, sister," the blonde called. "Can't trust cops."

"You're right about that."

"Taking advice from drunks now, Addy?"

"I trust her more than I trust you."

"We've gotta stick together," the drunk said.

Liberty turned to the other cell. "Shut up or I'll see to it that you spend extra time drying out in there."

The blonde made an obscene gesture with her finger, but kept quiet.

"Why don't you tell me what you're up to," Liberty coaxed. "There's no point in keeping it a secret any longer."

"I have no idea what you're talking about. I've told you and the others, I don't know anything about that reporter or about any radioactivity. Neither does Tommy. How many more times can I say it?"

"Until you tell me what I want to hear." Liberty's face turned ugly and she stepped closer to the bars. "You said before that you didn't know anything about it, which wasn't true. You and Tommy are the only possibilities and the only suspects. And the camera in your possession is the clincher. Now where is the film?"

Addy stared at her. "There's no film in the camera?"

"You know there wasn't. Where is it?"

Addy sat wearily on the cot and dropped her head to her hands. The film could have possibly exonerated her and Tommy, but now even that hope was gone.

"I don't know."

"Hah. The film contains incriminating evidence against you, and you've destroyed it. But you know what? It doesn't matter. I'm confident we can convict without it." Liberty stepped away from the bars. "In the morning, I plan to ask the judge to deny bail. I'll say you pose a possible flight risk and keep you here until you confess."

She walked away with loud steps, but Addy didn't look up. Holding her throbbing head and massaging her temples didn't help. The evidence did seem to point her way, but surely no one would believe it. How long could they keep her here? What must Tommy be going through? She had failed him, and failed her grandmother's trust in her. She was in the worst situation of her life with no one to rely on.

"Don't suppose you'd want to share a piece of that nut bread," the blonde said. "The food in here is garbage."

Addy cut the loaf in half, but before she hit bottom, her fork struck something metallic. Curious, she dug into the bread and extracted a fingernail file. Fern was a big fan of old black-and-white movies, but the file would only be useful for a manicure.

❖

Karen climbed the old oak, and as she waited for the door to open, she noticed that Dale and his associate would completely finish the house soon. But poor Addy might not be here to see it. The door swung open and Jeff Olson meandered past, a glob of peanut butter stuck to the corner of his mouth. For a moment, she panicked.

"Is Tommy here?"

Jeff looked at her quizzically. "'Course. Where else would he be?"

Karen sighed and went inside. Tommy sat at the table eating a PB and J sandwich. His face brightened.

"You want a sandwich? Jeff made them. He's a really good cook."

Karen smiled. "I'm sure he is, but no thanks. I need to talk with Tommy, Jeff. Alone."

"Okay. You gonna ask him about the dead guy?"

"Yes." Karen cringed. Kids were so blunt about such things, probably from so much television, where death and mayhem were an everyday occurrence.

"I'll go help my brother. Maybe I can get some extra money to buy that new Doctor Doom comic." Jeff walked out on the deck, but before closing the door, he stuck his head back in. "Oh, and don't forget to ask Officer Kaczarowski how to work that camera, Tommy. She knows all about that kind of stuff."

He closed the door and Karen stood motionless. "What camera?"

Tommy avoided her gaze, but she took his shoulders.

"What camera is Jeff talking about? This is important, Tommy. Please, tell me."

Tommy toyed with his sandwich, seeming lost in thought. "I found a camera."

Karen sat down at the table and pushed his plate out of reach. "Where? Where did you find it?"

"I know I was supposed to give it back," Tommy whined. "It didn't belong to me, but I was only playing with it."

"It's okay. What did you do with the camera, Tommy? Where is it now?"

"I hid it in Grandma's closet, with all the other stuff. I didn't think anybody would find it there."

Karen leaned back slowly in her chair, her mind racing. Addy didn't know anything about the camera after all. It still took Karen some time to realize that Tommy came and went at will, leaving his tree house when everyone continued to believe he didn't. Until she adjusted to that reality, she would continue to underestimate him.

"Am I in trouble?" Tommy asked mournfully.

"No, but it's really important that you tell the truth. I need to know everything so I can help Addy."

"When is Addy coming home? Is she going away again for a long time like before?" Tommy's eyes filled with tears and his lower lip trembled.

Karen didn't want to worry him, but she also needed to prepare him just in case.

"I'm trying to help Addy, Tommy. If you tell me the truth about the man you found, I can. Now tell me exactly what happened that night."

❖

It was late when Karen entered the county jail and headed toward Addy's cell. She was tired, but she needed to ease Addy's mind about the camera.

"Oh, Tommy," Addy said when she'd heard the whole story. "He couldn't have known what he was doing."

"Probably not. But it still looks bad for him. The DA could make a case that Tommy wanted the camera and killed Vinson for it."

"That's absurd."

"I know, but until we find out what's going on, the circumstantial evidence is overwhelming."

Addy reached through the bars and gripped Karen's hands. "You can't let them take Tommy away for something he didn't do. Please."

Karen took Addy's hands and brought them to her lips, kissing them lightly. Holding Addy's gaze, she tried to strengthen her and convince her that she was on her side.

"I'll do everything I can, I promise."

Tears slowly ran down Addy's cheeks as she pressed the side of her face to the bars. "I don't know what I'd do without you. Thank you. I'm sorry I wasted so many years holding a grudge."

Karen continued to clasp Addy's hands, wishing she could put her arms around her and tell her she wouldn't let anything bad happen to either her or Tommy. But she couldn't do that until she could discover the true culprits. Each time she learned something new about the crime, the evidence seemed to point at the Coopers. Who else could be responsible, not only for Vinson's death, but for the environmental angle? She dismissed Fern and Chauncey outright, but who did that leave?

"Hey, isn't it against the law to fraternize with the prisoners?"

The blond alcoholic had sobered during the day and become increasingly cantankerous.

"You've got me as a witness, honey. I'll swear the deputy was harassing you."

Addy suppressed a grin but didn't release Karen's hands. Even if she was let out of jail, she wouldn't know how to repudiate the accusations against her and Tommy. She gazed into Karen's steady blue eyes and wished that the thick, solid bars of her cell would miraculously disappear.

"I'd better go," Karen said hoarsely.

Addy could only nod, and slowly Karen removed her hands and stepped away. For a moment, Addy almost asked her to stay, but finally Karen turned her back and was gone.

Chapter Twenty-six

H oly shit," Frank muttered.

Abel looked up from his corn flakes at Frank, who was reading the newspaper. His face had turned deathly pale, and Abel knew it couldn't be good news. Frank jumped up from the kitchen table and rushed to his office, shouting commands at him and Clarence.

"We've got to dump this stuff now."

Abel followed him nervously. "What's going on, Frank?"

Frank began tossing equipment and wires into a duffel bag. "The cops found a camera in the Cooper house. They think it belongs to the reporter."

Abel's heart skipped a lot of beats and his spoon froze in midair. He opened his mouth to speak, but nothing came out.

"Fuck." Clarence's eyes opened wide like a cartoon character's. "I'm outta here."

Clarence was about to run out of the room, but Frank grabbed him by the collar and growled, "Where the hell do you think you're going?"

"That reporter took pictures of us. Where the hell do you think I'm going? The cops could be pulling up any minute. I'm heading for Canada."

"Oh, well, that's a perfectly safe place to run to," Frank said, like he was mocking Clarence.

"Well, what are you gonna do, then?" Clarence acted like he was going to stick out his tongue at Frank.

"We don't know what the cops have, and I'm going to find out. Here." Frank handed him the duffel bag. "You and Abel take this and get rid of it. I'm driving to the courthouse to see what I can find out."

"Somebody could recognize you," Abel said. His brother was so brave.

"No one is going to be looking for me at the courthouse. If anything, they'll be headed here. You two take off and head for the boat, get rid of that stuff, and then lay low. I'll call you on your cell when I know something."

Clarence grabbed the duffel and headed out the door.

Abel followed him, but paused in the doorway. "Be careful, Frank."

He hurried down the porch steps to Clarence's waiting car, where Clarence spun out in the driveway and raced toward the highway, a trail of dust obscuring them from view. Frank smiled. The kid had the camera all this time. He knew it. But it didn't make any sense. Then again, the kid was nuts. The Cooper boy didn't want to blackmail them. He was just hiding it. But he must have had the smarts to turn it over to the cops. Damn. Why hadn't he searched the tree house? It was too late now. He could get rid of the kid, but the film would put the noose around his neck anyway if the pictures showed what he was afraid they would—him building a dirty bomb.

He had to find out for sure. Glancing around the house one last time to make sure he hadn't missed anything, he grabbed his car keys and headed for town.

❖

"Bail is set at two hundred and fifty thousand dollars. Next case."

Addy stood before the judge and cast a grateful look at

Karen. If it hadn't been for Karen's testimony, and the fact that the judge was her cousin's wife, Addy would still be counting the water stains on the ceiling of her cell. After the bondsman posted Addy's bail, which Karen had co-signed, the judge dismissed her and they filed out of the courtroom, stepping quickly onto the sunny sidewalk.

She was free, and she felt so giddy she almost laughed. Despite the charges and the intensity with which the prosecutor had pursued them, the judge had determined that any number of individuals could have placed the camera in the house and that unless more substantial evidence could be brought to bear, Addy was out on bail pending her trial. She thanked her court-appointed attorney, a middle-aged balding man who spoke with a lisp but made up for it with his energetic defense, and strolled beside Karen to her car.

"Would you like to go someplace and celebrate?"

Addy shook her head. "There's nothing to celebrate…yet. The trial is soon. To be honest, I just want to go home and see Tommy."

Karen nodded and helped her into the car. As they drove, their silence was heavy with unspoken words. Addy tentatively reached across the seat and laid her hand over Karen's after a few blocks, relieved when Karen gripped it tight. The connection grounded her and kept her from losing control. If she dwelt on her situation, she would fall apart. Right now, she needed to be strong, for Tommy if not for herself.

Fern came bustling out the front door when they pulled up, wiping her hands on a dish towel.

"I've made blueberry pancakes to welcome you home. Chauncey is out back churning the ice-cream maker, and Tommy is…well, in his usual place."

Addy was so glad to be back home and out of jail. They entered the house, and Karen continued to the backyard. Addy lingered in the kitchen, appreciating the warm room and luxuriating in the familiar safety.

"Did you really get out on bail, or did the file come in handy?" Fern asked, glancing out back.

Addy smiled. "I appreciate your support, Fern, really I do. But I got out of jail the legal way. I can't leave town, and I'm only free while everyone prepares for the trial."

Fern whispered, "I've been speaking with Chauncey. He says he has a cousin in Matamoros who does odd jobs in Brownsville, Texas. He can get you as far south as Veracruz. From there, we can get you to Cancun, where Chauncey's family lives. You could take a boat across to Cuba and they'd never find you."

"Thanks, Fern, but I've got to think of Tommy, remember?"

"I'm working on that." She frowned. "Maybe we can ship some trees to Mexico so Tommy would feel at home on his voyage. Once Tommy's there, he can cross the country like Tarzan, swinging through the jungle."

Addy stared at Fern, wondering if she was serious or had truly lost her mind. Before she could answer, Karen stepped through the screen door.

"Tommy's fine, but he's asking for you."

Addy excused herself and climbed the tree. Seeing Tommy again made her realize she really was home, and she hugged him close.

"Are you here for good this time?"

The mournful sound of his voice nearly tore Addy's heart from her chest. She wished she could reassure him, but she didn't know how long she'd be home. At the very least she would be back in court. At the worst, she'd be in prison for life. They sat down on the bed.

"I'm home now," she said. "What have you been up to since I've been gone?"

"I learned a new bird call," he announced proudly. "Mr. Velasquez taught me the toucan's song." He pursed his lips and trilled out a series of rasping notes.

"That's very nice."

"Then yesterday, Jeff came over and spent the night. We played hide-and-seek in the tree for a while, and then it got dark."

Addy was about to say something, but Tommy's words made her pause. What struck her as odd?

"What did you say?"

"Jeff spent the night."

"No, you said...you said you played hide-and-seek?"

Tommy nodded.

The memory crashed in on Addy as she remembered the night she had found Tommy near the shore in the tall weedy grass. He was standing next to the body saying something similar, about men playing hide-and-seek and the man with the camera. She jumped from the bed, shaking excitedly. Running to the window, she shouted, "Karen!"

❖

"Where are we going?" Abel asked, cupping the flame of his lighter against the wind.

Clarence steered the forty-six-foot Harper-Jones fishing boat out of the harbor and into the open Chesapeake. Her twin Caterpillar diesel engines chugged noisily as they churned in the water, the waves spraying lightly over the bow. The boat had belonged to Frank's army buddy, Wayne Newton, who had left Frank the keys.

"Far enough out where no one can see us."

"Then what?" Abel stared at him. Clarence made him nervous. He was unpredictable, and Abel didn't trust him. The big oaf was also stupid, and that scared him even more.

"We're dumping this shit overboard into deep water where no one will ever find it."

"But what if Frank wants it back?" Abel was very nervous now. Clarence was one thing, but Frank's anger was something else altogether. If Frank had only meant to have them hide his equipment in order to return it to him when things cooled off, he'd probably kill them if he found out they had dumped it in the bottom of the ocean.

"He said to get rid of it, and that's what I'm doing. If he wants it back, he'll have to jump in and get it." Clarence laughed like a maniac, then shifted into idle. Walking to the stern, he picked up the duffel bag and pitched it into the blue waters of the Chesapeake.

❖

Frank waited outside the jail as reporters hovered nearby. They had arrived late in the day, not realizing that Addy Cooper had already made bail. They were trying to interview the DA or anyone who happened to come out of the building who might know something about the murder investigation. Someone in a suit came out onto the steps, and the reporters rushed him, obscuring him with cameras and microphones. Frank hung back, awaiting the outcome.

The man obviously knew nothing, but enjoyed the attention he was receiving. He blathered on until Frank noticed a bleached blonde exiting the jail, accompanied by a man in a cheap suit who looked like a public defender. They parted company and the woman stumbled down the steps, pausing to adjust her disheveled appearance. She was about to divert her path toward the reporters when Frank stepped up and took her by the arm.

"Hey," she protested.

Frank walked her around the corner of the building. If his hunch was right, the woman had recently spent time in jail.

"Excuse me, ma'am," he said. "I'm Bob Smith of the *Post*, and I want to ask you a few questions, if you don't mind."

The woman straightened immediately. "If this is about the woman who killed the reporter, I'm the one you need to talk to. I shared a cell with her. She confessed the whole crime to me."

Frank eyed her skeptically, but played along.

"Really? Then you're the woman I want. Of course, the *Post* will be happy to pay for your story."

The woman's bloodshot eyes brightened noticeably. "How much?"

"Would five hundred be sufficient?"

The amount had its intended effect. The woman nearly tripped all over herself to tell Frank her story. He listened impatiently, knowing that most of what she said was either outright lies or greatly embellished. Unable to take anymore of her gibberish, he interrupted smoothly.

"Did she ever talk about a camera while you were there?"

The blonde squinted. After a few minutes, however, she snapped her fingers as a low-wattage light bulb seemed to flicker on.

"Yes, as a matter of fact, she did. Some cop was asking her about it."

Frank's pulse quickened. "Think very hard. What did she say? This is important and could be worth a lot more money than what we're offering."

"I remember exactly what she said. By that time, I was pretty sober—I mean, I had just woken up and was paying close attention. The cop was asking her about the film. They couldn't find it and wanted to know what she did with it. But she said she didn't know anything about it."

Frank only half listened after that. His mind flew back to the kid in the tree house. He had it all along. No one else would think to look for it there—everyone's attention was focused on the girl.

The woman had stopped talking and waited expectantly. He thanked her for the information and wrote down her name and address, telling her that his newspaper would send her a check in the mail. As he limped down the street to his car, he tossed the slip of paper with her address into the trash can at the curb.

CHAPTER TWENTY-SEVEN

Liberty was furious that Addy had been released into the deputy's custody the day before. No longer able to question her suspect, she focused on the environmental aspects of the case. After all, that was her primary concern, not the reporter's death. Addy had definitely committed the crime and her brother was mixed up in it as well, but Liberty needed to reexamine the radioactive waste in the Chesapeake and determine its components precisely. If she could tie that situation in with what had gone on at Addy's former workplace, she could get a solid conviction.

"Girls Just Want to Have Fun" rang from the cell case on her hip, and she flipped open her phone.

"Liberty."

"We just got a call from the EPA. Radioactive levels around Deale have spiked. They're on their way via the scientific vessel *Ship of Fools* and will use all the resources available to examine the waters around Deale and give us immediate answers."

"When did this happen?"

"Very suddenly, within the last twenty-four hours, but they won't know for sure until they examine the waters and begin cleanup activity. If this isn't stopped right now, and word leaks out to the press, it will cause a major panic in the area. If the terrorists plan to poison the watershed that provides drinking water to DC, we can't do a lot to stop them."

"I'll stop them. I know exactly who's responsible. I just need to get the proof. Book me a flight to Oakland, California."

❖

"We have to find out who the men are, so let's have Tommy look at some photos."

Karen sat at the kitchen table with Cheatham and Grassley, who had been at the station late that afternoon when Karen called in. They had tried to contact Liberty but were only able to leave a voice message. It wasn't like her to be unavailable, and no one knew exactly where she was. But they were certain she was investigating clues about the perpetrators.

Cheatham and Grassley had listened to Tommy's somewhat convoluted story and said they weren't sure what to believe, but if Tommy was right, they were trying to locate three Caucasian males, possibly the Gripps. The crime was taking on a whole new dimension. They said they would quit interrogating Addy and Tommy and instead focus on the three men in the house across the inlet. The theory that the Gripps were involved was plausible.

Addy was making a pot of coffee and occasionally stared out the window to the red oak. Tommy was on the deck, his binoculars focused toward the inlet. She had allowed the agents to talk with Tommy, but all he would say was that one was a snipe, one a pelican, and the other a sandpiper. She didn't think the information would help them find the suspects. They should be showing Tommy a book on Maryland wildlife instead of mug shots.

"You can bring the photos here, right?" Addy asked. "Tommy doesn't have to go to the police station, does he?"

Karen shook her head. "No. It'll be fine, I promise."

She rose and approached Addy at the kitchen sink. Though

Karen acted like she wanted to touch her, she only said that she better stay around because the publicity surrounding Addy's arrest had made the papers. If those guys were still in the area, they might want to pay Addy and Tommy a call tonight.

"We'll make a game of it," Karen said. "Tommy will have a good time and not suspect a thing. But, Addy, we need his help desperately. One man has already been killed, and we don't know what we're up against."

The men seated at the table waited with expectant looks on their faces. Meeting Karen's gaze, Addy nodded, so the agents rose and said they'd be back in the morning with the photos. After they left, being in the kitchen alone with Karen made her nervous, so she busied herself with the coffeemaker, flipping the off switch to on, and the coffee began to drip. Karen hadn't moved away and heat waves emanated from her, but Addy tried very hard to ignore them.

"Just sugar, right?" she asked.

"Right."

As Addy scooped two spoonfuls of sugar into a mug and poured the coffee, her hand shook, and she gripped the handle tight.

"Here, let me get that." Karen put her hands over Addy's to steady the pot.

Addy wished she hadn't done that. What began as a slight tremble in her hands turned into uncontrollable shaking all the way to her knees. She was simply tired, she decided, raw and vulnerable—still recovering from Liberty's stinging betrayal. And even though her relationship with Karen appeared to be improving, she wasn't sure where they were headed. They couldn't simply pick up where they left off, but maybe they could start anew. She wasn't sure if that was the right thing to do, but her body sure liked the idea.

She released the coffeepot and Karen poured them both a cup. But neither of them paid any attention to it. Addy tried to look everywhere but at Karen, knowing if she did look at her, she wouldn't be able to control her reaction. She had too much to do and worry about. But when she finally met Karen's steady gaze, she was lost.

"I've missed you so much, Addy." Karen stroked her cheek. "Please, let me love you the way you need to be loved. It's all I've ever wanted."

Addy closed her eyes at the touch. She had no strength to resist it anyway, and she simply gave in. Even with her eyes shut, she could feel Karen drawing closer until their lips met. Their kiss was so much better than she remembered, and she floated away on a cloud of euphoria. Suddenly, Karen lifted her and carried her into her bedroom, their connection not breaking until she laid her on the bed.

They made love well into the night, slowly, as though now would last forever. Addy had dreamt so often of this, of being with Karen again, and had wondered whether it would feel the same as she remembered. Her memories didn't compare to what she was experiencing—the way Karen touched her, how their bodies fit like they were made for one another. Karen stroked her gently when she needed it, withholding pleasure to heighten her need, then giving her all to push Addy to climax. Karen played Addy's body like a virtuoso, and Addy hummed in tune.

❖

"We can't go back there, Frank," Abel said. "They're looking for us right now."

"They're looking for someone, but not us, and certainly not on this boat," Frank said. "They don't have the film, but the boy has it and we have to get it back."

"You don't know that for sure," Abel whined.

"My gut knows it, and that's good enough for me."

"Well, it's not good enough for me," Clarence said. "You're as fruity as the kid if you think I'm going back up that tree. I've loaded up my car with my stuff and I'm heading to Canada. If you want to come along, that's up to you, but either way, I'm outta here."

"And they'll catch you at the border," Frank said. "If we don't get the film back, they'll track you down like a dog. You won't last a minute out there. But if we get our hands on it, we're safe. They'll never know who did it."

Clarence studied Frank skeptically, but a glimmer of doubt flashed across his eyes.

"I don't know…" he said slowly.

"Either you're with me or you're dead. Take your pick. It doesn't matter to me if they catch your lazy ass. But I know you, Clarence. You'll squeal like Ned Beatty in *Deliverance* if they get hold of you. So you're coming with me whether you like it or not. Now, grease up your face and let's go."

Frank finished blackening his face, then checked to see if they were following suit. Abel and Clarence gazed nervously at each other, but slowly picked up the can of grease and smeared some on their faces. Frank grinned. They'd do as he said, because they knew he was right. Abel would obey, even if he didn't really like the plan. But Frank still wasn't sure he could trust Clarence. If he did anything he wasn't supposed to, Frank might have to stop him—in any way he felt necessary.

When their faces were dark, they dressed in black and steeled themselves for the night ahead. Frank took the stern of the boat and headed inland to the inlet that led to the Coopers'. The running lights were off so no one would see them. The sky was overcast, so even the boat's outline against the horizon wouldn't be noticeable. Only the diesel engines were audible, and he hoped no one would be outside this late, because the noise carried a great distance across the water. As if in answer to his prayers, a bolt of lightning briefly lit up the sky, followed moments later by a rumble of thunder. The storm would cover their approach, and Frank smiled broadly.

❖

Liberty was about to board her plane at BWI for Oakland when "Girls Just Want to Have Fun" jingled at her side again.

"Liberty."

"Get your ass back to Deale," her handler yelled. "There's a new lead, and Cheatham and Grassley are on the move. They did a background check on the Gripp family. Seems Francis James Gripp is former Special Forces with more than a grudge against the military."

"That can't be. They're crazy. It's the Cooper woman, I tell you. I'm sure of it."

"Then go on to Oakland if you want. But the two agents just paid a visit to the Gripps, who apparently cleaned house and left. No one knows where they went."

"Shit. I'm on my way."

Liberty ran out of the terminal to the median, where she managed to hop on a shuttle leaving for the rental-car agency. If Cheatham and Grassley got the collar and it turned out that the Gripps were involved, she'd wind up with egg on her face. That couldn't happen. This was her case and nobody was taking it away from her.

The Gripps were probably Addy's means to an end—in on it to help her achieve her goals. Liberty just knew Addy was the brains behind this whole mess.

Chapter Twenty-eight

Addy marveled at Karen lying next to her, the light from the hallway streaming through the cracks around the door. The window was slightly open and the breeze rocked the blinds in and out. The impending storm had stirred up a damp, dank odor from the vegetation and made the salt air heavy and thick.

But Karen commanded her attention, and for the first time in a long while, Addy felt at peace. Karen was still as beautiful as she remembered, with only a few minor lines around her eyes, signs of the sun rather than of age. And if Addy concentrated very hard, she could almost imagine that it was six years earlier and Karen was her entire world.

"What are you thinking?" Karen murmured.

Addy had believed Karen was asleep and that she observed her unknowingly. Should she tell Karen the truth, or were her feelings too new even for her to completely understand?

"I've been thinking about how much my life has changed so quickly. I'm back home in Deale, with this house and Tommy, and a new life. I thought things were going so well, and then this whole mess with the reporter and Liberty and God knows what else happened. Sometimes I can't imagine ever getting my life on track, and then something miraculous occurs. You step in and make everything all right again."

She gestured to the two of them in bed together. Never had

she dreamed this would happen again, yet it felt as natural to be with Karen as if time had never passed. She sighed, wishing she could close out the rest of the world and not move from this warmth and tranquility.

"I didn't always come to your support," Karen said.

"But you always believed in my innocence, and you never gave up on me. Not many people did."

"Fern and Chauncey were always there. And Dee-Dee has been too. She misses you and would love to see you again. But she's afraid you don't want her around."

Addy averted her eyes. "I know. I was hard on her. It wasn't fair of me to judge what happened in the past. It's over and done with. We all need to move on. I'll go see her tomorrow and try to make amends."

❖

Frank cut the engines on the small fishing boat and let it glide close to shore. After Abel quietly lowered the anchor in about fifteen feet of water they prepared to go ashore. Frank wanted to search the tree house for the film, and if they found it, they'd get rid of the crazy guy. If not, they'd take him with them and force him to tell them where it was. Either way, they'd eliminate the only witness. Frank had done it before, and he'd do it again. He wasn't about to give up now that he was so close to getting his revenge on the government.

"Let's go," he said.

He slipped into the water first and Clarence and Abel quickly followed.

"Holy shit, this water's cold." Clarence's teeth were chattering.

"Shut up. I told you, no talking until this is over. Sound carries over water."

"Oh, oh, I think I've got a leg cramp." Abel splashed noisily.

"Jesus Christ."

Frank grabbed Abel by the collar and dragged him to shallow water.

"Stand up, you idiot. Now everybody shut up and let's get this thing done."

They waded to dry land and squished their way toward the Cooper house. A flash of lightning made them duck and drop to their knees. When a crack of thunder followed, they used the noise as cover to race inland to the safety of the woods. Following the tree line, they approached the red oak tree thirty yards away.

Frank led the way up the tree and, to his surprise, found the door to the tree house unlocked. Signaling them to silence, he slowly turned the knob and went in. It was even darker inside, but he didn't dare turn on a light. Anyone could be watching from the main house, and he didn't want to draw attention. Feeling his way toward the back of the room, he was almost where he remembered the bed to be when something crashed behind him. He spun around, but as he did, he knocked over a floor lamp that also clunked to the floor. Somebody shouted, and Frank began to run.

❖

A muffled crash from outside distracted Addy from Karen's tongue, lazily tracing a line from the inside of her thigh upward. She didn't want Karen to stop, but perhaps she should find out what had caused the sound.

"Karen."

"Hmm?" Karen didn't slow in her path to victory. "Too fast?"

Her tongue came dangerously close to the point of no return, but more noises from outside concerned Addy. She gently pushed Karen's head out of the way and sat up.

"What was that?"

"What was what? I didn't hear a thing. Come on, baby,

we're so close." Karen was reaching for Addy when a definite yelp sounded from the tree house.

"Something's wrong with Tommy." Addy crawled out of bed and reached for her robe.

They raced into the living room as Fern came stomping down the stairs, wire curlers in her hair and a baseball bat in her hand. Right behind her was Chauncey, clad only in an undershirt and boxer shorts. Fern wore a revealing nightgown that left nothing to the imagination, and Addy had to look away.

"What in Sam Hill is going on?" Fern shouted.

"It's Tommy," Addy tossed over her shoulder as she ran out the back door.

Before Karen could add anything, a loud pounding at the front door caused them all to jump. Karen flung the door open, not really caring who it was in her hurry to get to the backyard. She was shocked to see Liberty on the front porch, whereas Liberty seemed to be surprised that the entire household was up and awake, but she stepped into the house anyway.

"What the hell are you doing here?" Karen said.

"I need to talk to Tommy again."

"Come on, then," Karen called as she ran to the back of the house.

"What's going on?"

"I think it's burglars." Fern tapped the baseball bat in her open palm. "But I've dealt with my share of scoundrels before."

"The Gripps," Liberty said.

"What?"

"Come on, Fern." Liberty ran toward the back of the house, and Fern and Chauncey followed her. They burst into the yard just as several dark figures scrambled down the tree.

"There," Fern shouted, then tripped over her nightgown, sending her headlong into Chauncey.

Liberty and Karen ran after the intruders while Addy headed for the tree. She raced up and into the house, flipping on a light.

The room was in shambles, with broken glass and a lamp strewn across the floor.

"Tommy," Addy yelled, beginning to sift through the wreckage. "Tommy, where are you?"

She panicked as she tossed objects out of her way. The place was too small to hide anyone, and when she finally looked under the bed and still couldn't find him, she collapsed on the floor in desperation.

Chauncey entered the kitchen. "Tommy?" he asked, his face betraying his bewilderment.

Addy shook her head, unable to speak for the choking sensation in her throat. But she didn't have time to cry. She had to find him. She struggled from her place on the floor and stumbled to the door. Fern waited below, baseball bat still in hand.

"Is Tommy okay?" she asked.

"He's gone."

❖

Liberty flew through the woods, trying to keep the intruders in sight, and periodic flashes of lightning helped. She vaguely recollected the layout of the Cooper property, recalling the path that wound to the shore. But racing through the unknown terrain left her uneasy. She had no backup save the deputy, who wasn't even armed, and she didn't know for certain how many bad guys they were chasing. At any moment, one of them could circle around behind them and take them down. Karen was stumbling along behind her, barefoot and barely dressed, and Liberty realized she would be no help whatsoever. *What a hick.*

The thunderclaps covered the intruders' escape, and after several minutes of running, Liberty lost them in the darkness. She stopped behind a stand of pines and motioned the deputy to her side. Panting, she gestured that she wanted to sweep around the last spot she'd seen them, trying to encircle them and flush them out of hiding. Karen nodded and fanned out toward the water while Liberty headed deeper into the woods.

❖

Clarence was on his knees, his arm flung around a fallen tree trunk, trying to catch his breath. Frank stared at him, disgusted. If he had his druthers, he'd leave the moron behind. But his half-baked cousin wouldn't last two seconds in the hands of an interrogator, and Frank wasn't about to let any of them be captured. Abel was no better, gasping against an oak tree. His two-pack-a-day habit had left him badly out of shape.

"Get up. We've got to get back to the boat."

"They'll see us in the water without the trees to hide us," Abel protested.

"It's our ticket out of here," Frank said. "We can't run in the woods forever. We don't know how many of them there are. If you want to stay here, fine. But I'm getting on that boat."

Clarence and Abel peeked at one another, then followed Frank toward the water. At the same time, the skies opened and a deluge began. Soaked and miserable, Frank was actually glad that it had finally started raining. It would decrease visibility and cover the sound of their movement. Once in the boat, they were home free.

❖

"Tommy," Addy shouted, running as fast as she could toward the water. She had no clue where he could be, but she stumbled blindly in the direction of the only place she guessed he might go. What if he wasn't alone, if he was hurt or being hurt by someone involved in the Vinson murder. If she hadn't been so determined to find him, she would have flown apart in a million pieces. She ran faster, her legs burning with the effort, but she refused to stop.

She was approaching the spot where Tommy had tried to bury the reporter when someone tackled her from behind. Screaming, she fell headlong into the tall grass, the damp ground cushioning her fall. Tight arms held on to her waist, and she struggled to escape her attacker's grip.

"Shh, Addy, it's me," Karen rasped.

Addy was so relieved it wasn't a criminal but rather someone she could trust that she sobbed and clutched at Karen's shoulders.

"Tommy's missing," she wailed. "Where is he, Karen? Help me. I've got to find him."

She started to get up, but Karen pinned her to the ground.

"Stay down. We don't know how many of them there are, and they could be armed."

"But I've got to help Tommy. Please, don't let them take him."

"I won't, but you have to stay put."

Karen held on to Addy, not wanting to release her. She was afraid Addy might get hurt, and the possibility tortured her. Now that she had Addy back, she couldn't lose her again. Knowing she had to get up and help Liberty, she reluctantly climbed to her feet.

"I'll be back," she said.

As she disappeared into the weeds and grass, Addy's anxiety increased. She couldn't bear for Karen to expose herself to danger. She had finally rediscovered her love for the one person who had ever meant anything to her, and the possibility of losing Karen overwhelmed her. For a few heartbeats Addy lay in the wet grass, the moisture from below and the pelting rain from above chilling her.

She was frustrated that she couldn't do anything and impatient to be merely waiting. Surely she could help. Rising to a crouched position, she peeked over the tops of the weedy grass but couldn't see or hear anything. With a burst of adrenaline, she ran toward the water.

CHAPTER TWENTY-NINE

Tommy wandered around in the cabin of the boat, enjoying the gentle rocking motion that the waves created. All the dials and controls in the cockpit fascinated him, and he sat in the captain's chair, playing with the wheel. The rain drummed on the roof and deck around him, but he felt warm and safe. In some ways, the boat reminded him of his house, nice and cozy, with everything he needed close at hand. But the boat reminded him of something else, something far away in his memory. Another boat during another time, his father smiling down at him.

It was a day much like this one, warm but rainy, and Tommy had been afraid out on the open water. His father had handled the boat like he knew what he was doing, though, slicing through the waves and laughing. Curious why his father wasn't afraid, Tommy crawled up from below deck to stand timidly by his side. Gradually, Tommy stopped quivering and the spray hit his face. He looked up at his father, who laughed again to see him soaking wet, like it was the funniest thing he'd ever seen. Encouraged by his father's laughter, Tommy smiled and relaxed. If his father was happy, everything must be all right, and the angry sky and choppy water no longer frightened him.

Now Tommy looked down at the console and discovered that the keys were still in the ignition. He remembered how his father had started the engine in their boat, so he turned the key and the engines roared. The sound startled him at first, but when the lights on the console lit up, it was like Christmas, full of red and green.

❖

Frank heard a noise like a car, no, a truck, but not quite. As he hobbled to the shore, his leg screaming with pain, he realized that it was the twin diesels on his boat. He had turned them off before they disembarked, so how could they possibly be on now? Where were the cops who were chasing them? They couldn't possibly have gotten in front of them and made it to the boat first. They didn't even know it was there.

"What the hell?" he shouted.

Fortunately, a crack of thunder disguised his voice, but his anger remained.

"What is it, Frank?" Abel ran up beside him and into the water. "How come our boat is running, Frank?"

Clarence pulled up and splashed into the water. "What are we gonna do now, Frank?"

Frank turned to them and stared. Water dripped from his nose and a cold rivulet traveled down the back of his collar to his spine. How he'd ever figured he could do anything with these idiots was beyond him. Did he have to think of everything?

He stared at the boat again. Had the cops somehow found it beforehand? Yet he couldn't see a police boat, or anything else for that matter. They were being chased from behind and were now committed to the water, so their only chance was to get back on the boat. He hesitated only an instant, then plunged in and began to swim.

❖

Karen raced to the shore and joined Liberty on the beach as three figures in the ink-black water swam toward the boat.

"They're getting away," Liberty shouted. She raised her gun and fired two shots, which only made the swimmers dive under water.

Scanning the shore, Karen saw the Cooper boat down the coast at the dock, too far away to reach now. She stood helplessly as the intruders escaped. Footsteps behind her made her turn around, and Addy staggered toward them.

"I heard gunshots." Addy panted. "Where's Tommy?"

"I don't know, but I don't think he's out there." Karen gestured to the men in the water.

Someone yanked Addy's arms behind her, and she glanced over her shoulder to see Liberty gripping her wrists.

"You're under arrest," she barked.

"What?" Addy shrieked.

"What the hell are you doing?" Karen asked. "You know damn well Addy doesn't have anything to do with this."

"I don't know anything of the sort," Liberty said smugly. "And don't get in my way, Deputy. I know you have a *special* interest in this suspect. Any interference on your part and I'll have to assume you're involved as well."

Addy gazed out into the pouring rain, unable to discern where the sky ended and the sea began. She could barely make out a boat being tossed by the waves and three figures splashing toward it. Even though her hair was plastered to her head and the water cascaded down upon her, she could feel hot tears slide down her cheeks. Where was Tommy? What was going on and who were those men? Hopeless, wet, and tired, she broke down and sobbed.

Suddenly the engines on the boat roared to life and the boat took off. Addy stared unhappily toward it, knowing that perhaps the only chance she had of discovering what had happened to Tommy was leaving on that boat. The rain and her tears blurred her vision, but something in the water drew her attention and she blinked rapidly to clear her vision.

"They're still in the water," Karen said. "I don't get it."

"It's an accomplice," Liberty snapped. "He's leaving his buddies to fend for themselves."

The boat angled off out to sea, then abruptly changed course and headed toward shore.

"He's going to run over them," Karen shouted, and headed for the water.

"Karen, no," Addy screamed.

The swimmers dove under the waves, but at the last second, the boat spun in circles.

❖

Frank kicked to the surface, gasping for air and keeping his eye on the boat. What the hell was going on? He was positive he had turned off the engines before they left—had they malfunctioned? Surely not. And it couldn't be the cops. They would just come and arrest them. That left only one other possibility—the kid.

"What the fuck is going on?" Clarence shouted. "Somebody's tryin' to kill us."

"What're we gonna do, Frank?" Abel coughed and spit up water.

"Here it comes again," Frank said.

He dove as far as his lungs allowed and hoped the others had enough sense to do the same, then he scrambled for the surface once the boat had passed. For several minutes the game continued, with the boat circling and them diving. Finally, gasping and spluttering for air, Clarence began to swim for shore, and Abel followed him.

"Get back here," Frank shouted above the din of the engines.

But apparently neither Clarence nor Abel heard him. They were too busy swimming for their lives. After glancing at the boat barreling down on him, Frank hurried after them. But the boat was following him to shore, so he panicked and swam as fast as his bad leg allowed, swallowing salt water and choking his way to land. When his feet touched bottom, he stood and stumbled to the sand.

"The boat's not stopping," the deputy shouted, and she grabbed Frank by the arm and yanked him out of the way. The other woman shoved Abel and Clarence to the ground and the boat whined, its engines out of the water. It crashed into the tall grass and thudded to a stop, wedged between two loblolly pines, its engines still spinning noisily.

Addy watched Liberty pull herself up into the boat and disappear. Soon the engines stopped and the silence contrasted starkly to the dripping rain. In a few minutes Liberty reappeared, pulling Tommy by his shirt.

"Tommy." Addy ran to the side of the boat, and he leapt over the side and flung himself into her arms.

"What the hell is going on?" Karen asked.

"Tommy!" Fern clapped her hands and laughed. Her curlers bounced around her head like a Slinky, and Chauncey stood next to her, drenched and covered in mud and leaves from his forays into the woods.

Liberty eyed them all suspiciously, then announced, "Don't anybody move. You're all under arrest."

❖

"Are you insane?" Karen asked. "What are you talking about, McDonald? Who's under arrest?"

"All of you." Liberty gestured to everyone standing within the circle by the boat. "Including you, Deputy. I believe you're aiding and abetting Ms. Cooper and her brother. And I think Miss Bush and Mr. Velasquez are also somehow involved."

"I have no idea what you're talking about," Fern said with a huff. "You must have hit your head, Miss McDonald."

"I almost did, Miss Bush." Liberty pointed to the boat with her pistol. "Tommy was aiming the boat right at me but failed. Only through my quick thinking was I able to jump out of the way at the last minute. Otherwise, I'd be seriously injured, or worse."

The scrawny leader of the escapees started edging into the grass and weeds, but Liberty noticed him and pursued him as he plunged into the woods.

"That's far enough, Gripp," Cheatham muttered as he appeared and held a gun in his face.

As Liberty walked out of the shadows with Cheatham and Grassley, she faced the group of criminals and smiled at her fellow agents smugly.

"Gentlemen, I've captured the whole lot of them. Your timing is perfect. Let's take them in."

"This is ridiculous," Addy said. "We're all innocent, except for those men."

"Forget it," Liberty said. "Just give it up, Addy, and confess. It'll go easier on you."

"I—" Addy spluttered. Everyone began to shout and argue their innocence. She clung to Tommy, refusing to let him go.

"We found the film," Cheatham shouted, holding the canister up for all to see.

The clamor gradually petered out until all was silent and Cheatham repeated himself.

"That doesn't prove anything," Liberty and the leader of the three men said simultaneously. She stared at him.

"Not at the moment," Cheatham went on. "But very shortly, we should have the answers to who killed Scott Vinson."

❖

Addy sat at the bar in the Happy Harbor a week later, drinking her second Bloody Mary as Chauncey taught Tommy how to throw darts. Fern perched on a bar stool across from her, tossing down shots of Jim Beam and detailing the steps of how to repair a Harley carburetor to a tattooed woman next to her. Addy leaned back on her stool, knowing Karen was there to prevent her from falling.

"Man, and here I thought I knew all the gossip in town," Dee-Dee said. She pulled the lever back on a draft she was pulling and slid it in front of Karen.

"I'm just glad it's all over." Addy sighed as Karen's arms wrapped around her. "And it's so good to have Tommy back."

His quick toss of four darts circled the bull's eye perfectly. Tommy's curiosity had saved them all, for who knew if and when the Gripps would have returned to search for the film. The roll clearly showed them working on what the FBI called a "dirty bomb," intent on poisoning the Chesapeake watershed. Vinson had also managed to snap a few photos as he ran away from his pursuers. Addy shuddered.

"Are you all right?" Karen kissed the top of Addy's head.

Addy tilted back and looked up at her. "I am now."

"It's your turn," Tommy told Karen. He sat on her stool next to Addy and took a big gulp of his Coke.

"Are you okay?" Addy ruffled the hair on his forehead.

"Yeah. "This is a lot of fun. Can I do it again?"

"Anytime you like." Addy was thrilled to see him so happy. He had told her about his dream on the boat, and how he felt their father was there with him, guiding the boat. She didn't quite understand what it all meant, but she felt closer to Tommy than she had in years. And the fact that he was at the Happy Harbor, and not afraid, was nothing short of a miracle. They weren't alone anymore.

"And can I play with Chauncey too?"

"Of course, if he wants to. But why?"

"He's not very good," Tommy whispered. "But don't tell him, okay?"

Addy smiled. "Okay, I won't."

"Promise?"

"Promise."

About the Author

KI Thompson is the author of two novels, *House of Clouds* (2008 Indie Book Award and 2008 Golden Crown finalists) and *Heart of the Matter*. She also has short stories in the anthologies *Erotic Interludes* (2–5), *Fantasy: Untrue Stories of Lesbian Passion*, and *Best Lesbian Romance 2007* as well as *Best Lesbian Romance 2009*. Her forthcoming novel, *The Will to Wynne*, a historical romance set during the American Revolutionary War, is due out in 2010.

Books Available From Bold Strokes Books

Lake Effect Snow by C.P. Rowlands. News correspondent Annie T. Booker and FBI Agent Sarah Moore struggle to stay one step ahead of disaster as Annie's life becomes the war zone she once reported on. Eclipse EBook (978-1-60282-068-5)

Revision of Justice by John Morgan Wilson. Murder shifts into high gear propelling Benjamin Justice into a raging fire that consumes the Hollywood Hills, burning steadily toward the famous Hollywood Sign—and the identity of a cold-blooded killer. Gay Mystery. (978-1-60282-058-6)

I Dare You by Larkin Rose. Stripper by night, corporate raider by day, Kelsey's only looking for sex and power, until she meets a woman who stirs her heart and her body. (978-1-60282-030-2)

Truth Behind the Mask by Lesley Davis. Erith Baylor is drawn to Sentinel Pagan Osborne's quiet strength, but the secrets between them strain duty and family ties. (978-1-60282-029-6)

Cooper's Deale by KI Thompson. Two would-be lovers and a decidedly inopportune murder spell trouble for Addy Cooper, no matter which way the cards fall. (978-1-60282-028-9)

Romantic Interludes 1: Discovery ed. by Radclyffe and Stacia Seaman. An anthology of sensual, erotic contemporary love stories from the best-selling Bold Strokes authors. (978-1-60282-027-2)

A Guarded Heart by Jennifer Fulton. The last place FBI Special Agent Pat Roussel expects to find herself is assigned to an illicit private security gig baby-sitting a celebrity. (Ebook) (978-1-60282-067-8)

Saving Grace by Jennifer Fulton. Champion swimmer Dawn Beaumont, injured in a car crash she caused, flees to Moon Island, where scientist Grace Ramsay welcomes her. (Ebook) (978-1-60282-066-1)

The Sacred Shore by Jennifer Fulton. Successful tech industry survivor Merris Randall does not believe in love at first sight until she meets Olivia Pearce. (Ebook) (978-1-60282-065-4)

Passion Bay by Jennifer Fulton. Two women from different ends of the earth meet in paradise. Author's expanded edition. (Ebook) (978-1-60282-064-7)

Never Wake by Gabrielle Goldsby. After a brutal attack, Emma Webster becomes a self-sentenced prisoner inside her condo—until the world outside her window goes silent. (Ebook) (978-1-60282-063-0)

The Caretaker's Daughter by Gabrielle Goldsby. Against the backdrop of a nineteenth-century English country estate, two women struggle to find love. (Ebook) (978-1-60282-062-3)

Simple Justice by John Morgan Wilson. When a pretty-boy cokehead is murdered, former LA reporter Benjamin Justice and his reluctant new partner, Alexandra Templeton, must unveil the real killer. (978-1-60282-057-9)

Remember Tomorrow by Gabrielle Goldsby. Cees Bannigan and Arieanna Simon find that a successful relationship rests in remembering the mistakes of the past. (978-1-60282-026-5)

Put Away Wet by Susan Smith. Jocelyn "Joey" Fellows has just been savagely dumped—when she posts an online personal ad, she discovers more than just the great sex she expected. (978-1-60282-025-8)

Homecoming by Nell Stark. Sarah Storm loses everything that matters—family, future dreams, and love—will her new "straight" roommate cause Sarah to take a chance at happiness? (978-1-60282-024-1)

Falling Star by Gill McKnight. Solley Rayner hopes a few weeks with her family will help heal her shattered dreams, but she hasn't counted on meeting a woman who stirs her heart. (978-1-60282-023-4)

Lethal Affairs by Kim Baldwin and Xenia Alexiou. Elite operative Domino is no stranger to peril, but her investigation of journalist Hayley Ward will test more than her skills. (978-1-60282-022-7)

A Place to Rest by Erin Dutton. Sawyer Drake doesn't know what she wants from life until she meets Jori Diamantina—only trouble is, Jori doesn't seem to share her desire. (978-1-60282-021-0)